I0520466

# A compilation of Ethnic Stories

Published by Michael Frimpon

ISBN     978-0-9864211-5-0

# What's Inside

# Dedication

[Steve Wonder...that's what friends are for...]

This book is dedicated to some special people.

Rodolfo Hollander of the Dominican Republic.

Gloria Hinton of Richton, Mississippi.

Alexander Anderson of Richmond, Virginia.

Sam Adomako-Kyei of Fort Worth, Texas.

Albert Yaw Sarpong of Alexandria, Virginia.

Joseph Mensah-Ansah of Accra, Ghana.

Thanks for being such good friends over the ages.

# THE
# PRIMARY
# SCHOOL YEARS

# The Visit

A visit by the DC? That was big news. There was some idle chatter that the District Commissioner aka DC would pay an official visit to Sakasaka primary school. The pupils in the school were ecstatic. The teachers however, looked upon his visits with trepidation. On his previous visit, the no nonsense DC had publicly rebuked a teacher for flogging a boy for the cardinal sin of dirty uniform. There was a practice of inspecting schoolchildren for dirty bodies and uniforms. These were edicts from the Ministry of education. Unlike the children, the teachers knew that the Minister of Education was a bigger shot than the DC, and violating such rules were of more consequence than the DC's reprimands. The dilemma was that the teachers did not know how they could implement the "Cleanliness is Godliness doctrine" without wielding the cane. The streets were dusty, the school environment was unpaved, and the road smack by the school was untarred. There was dust everywhere. Therefore, trying to avoid dirt on the body was like

washing the water off fish. One thing was certain; there was no flogging during the DC's visits.

The DC had another habit that made the teachers uncomfortable. On his previous visits, he used to interview and pose questions to students he ran into on his visits. Sometimes he barged into classrooms while classes were in session and observed, but most times, he got involved. To ensure that the students were well prepared to answer the DC's unrehearsed questions, the teachers held special English classes to make sure randomly selected students would acquit themselves creditably if the DC ever called them. The kids were taught how to use common verbs, nouns, and pronouns. Nouns like chairs, tables, black board that were within eyesight in the classrooms were used to construct sentences.

A novel strategy of the teachers was to make sure identified dunces did not get into the cross hairs of the DC the next visit. They made a list of the weakest students and planned to inform each one individually that the DC's visit had been rescheduled to the following week, and that the day had been declared a holiday. That was not a very smart plan, but they trusted in the stupidity of the select group to not see through it; after all, they qualified

to be in that selection.

The day came, and Kojo had the extra sleep typical of holidays. He woke up and lazed about until he got bored. Then he decided to go to Patapaa's house only to be told the latter had left for school. Initially he laughed at his stupid cousin for going to school on a holiday. When he learnt the second friend and the third friend had all gone to school, he headed for the school premises. Disheveled he cast a look of a real dunce, which is what he was.

The DC came with a sizeable entourage to show that he was the monarch of all he surveyed. As was his custom, he barged straight into the classroom closest to him. Kojo entered almost at the same time as the DC. It was as if he was part of the big man's entourage. Whilst the children were giggling and envying Kojo for being in the DC's entourage, the look on the face of the teacher was of utter consternation. All the planning of the school authorities for an incident-free visit were now down the drain. Plan A was to equip the children with enough vocabulary to pass the DC's interviews; plan B was to ensure the dunces stayed away from the school during the DC's visit. Sadly, they did not craft Plan C. Plan C, the situation where the chief dunce was in class with the DC was what was happening in real time. The DC and

Kojo in one room meant fireworks.

DC: Children Jump. Boy in corner, what is the class doing?

Jaja: We are jumping.

DC: Clap. Girl in front here, what is the class doing?

Class: We are clapping.
DC: Hands up. Boy by window there, what is the class doing?

Kojo: We are 'handsing' up.

Teacher Polo wished he were anywhere but in class. The DC was glancing in his direction with a smirk on his face. The big man was not done yet. He was enjoying his teaching and the generally good answers. He chanced upon a broom languishing in the corner and blurted.

Girl in the center, pick up that thing. He beckoned the girl to sweep the floor.

DC: show by hands and tell me what she is doing.

The teacher almost collapsed when he saw Kojo's hand shoot up quickest.

Kojo: She is brooming the floor.

DC: Huh?

Kojo: She is sweeping the broom.

DC: Huh, huh?

**Kojo:** She is flooring the broom.

Mercifully, the bell tolled for recreation. By school rules, the children could not use the washroom until break, unless it was an emergency. They therefore held it in until the bell rang. Then not even the powerful DC could stop the mass of little bodies from sprinting to the 'first-come-first-served' toilets. Any delay or attempt to delay could result in unpleasant circumstances. The big man turned around to congratulate the teacher for the free concert he had witnessed; but the teacher recognizing the enmity of the fireworks had stolen out the room with the fleeing mayhem

# Things Fall Apart

Bewildered was an understatement. The DC was amazed that right in front him was an empty class. He was really enjoying himself with the children but now before him were empty chairs. Until that moment, he didn't know that a school bell was more powerful than a district commissioner. It was perhaps the first time in his recollection that the people he wanted to address had left his presence without his permission. He was mystified, astonished, perplexed, confused, befuddled, and bewildered. Nevertheless, he had just arrived so there would be plenty of time and opportunities to meet with his beloved audience of little children. The DC had enquired about the boy who had thoroughly entertained him the past few minutes and learnt his new friend's name was Kojo. As he stepped out of the classroom, he ran into some returnee children and spontaneously began to interact with them. Like a magnet that attracts metal, his first question went straight to Kojo.

**DC:** Kojo, who wrote Things Fall Apart?

Some of the headstrong students sometimes wrote graffiti on the walls of the school. Such students, if caught were severely punished. Nana, thinking that a student had written Things Fall Apart on the walls thus answered.

**Kojo:** Sir I did not write anything o. In fact, I was not in school in the morning because I was told it was a holiday.

Shocked, the DC turned to the teacher.

**DC:** Oh, my Lord? Teacher, can you believe the student does not know who wrote Things Fall apart?

The word 'wrote', for some reason evoked a comedic scene of someone writing something on any of the school walls, and neither student nor teacher or anybody else heard anything beyond the word. The nervous teacher, thinking the DC had observed a writing on a wall somewhere also gave an answer like Kojo's.

**Teacher:** Sir, I do not believe any of the students from my class wrote 'Things Fall Apart' on the wall because I always whip them when I catch them writing on the wall.

The exasperated DC made his way to the head teacher's office.

**DC:** Something is wrong. Both the students and the teacher do not know who wrote Things Fall Apart?

**Head teacher:** Honorable, I cannot believe one of the little devils

has managed to write 'Things Fall Apart' on the wall so soon after we repainted it for your visit. I will wring that little devil's neck as soon as I find him.

The DC did not know whether to laugh at the hilarities he was being treated to or be angry at the ignorance of people having no knowledge of the seminal book that he read in that same school eons ago. He turned to the deputy DC in his entourage and screamed.

**DC:** Deputy, can you believe none of the students, teachers and the head teacher know who wrote Things Fall Apart"?

**Deputy DC:** Calm down honorable, I witnessed everything. I think this situation calls for a committee to be set up to find the culprit wrote this. This is all propaganda by your enemies. The district is not falling apart.

The stunned DC just kept mute. He was not sure what could come out of his mouth if he uttered a word.

On his way home, he run into his pastor about to drive off.

**DC:** 'Man of God' Good day. Sorry to bother you but I just must get this off my chest.

**Pastor:** Yes, honorable get it off your chest, the Bible says......

**DC:** Can you believe the students, teachers, head teacher of

Sakasaka, and my own deputy do not know who wrote Things Fall Apart?

**Pastor:** The devil is a liar. Things are not falling apart and will not fall apart if I remain pastor of the church. That school is demon possessed and deliverance is what is needed. The enemy will not survive my prayers. In fact, I am commencing a 2-day prayer and fast beginning tomorrow; provided I can get a little er er kola.

The dumbstruck DC could not even continue the conversation. His mouth agape, he dipped into his pocket and fished out some bills. Straight to his home he went.

He caught his breath long enough to be able to vent unto his lovely wife, a well-educated woman with a Middle School Leaving Certificate aka MSLC.

**DC:** Darling you cannot believe what happened on my visit to the school today. The students did not know who wrote Things Fall Apart, the teachers neither, but the most shocking is that the so-called highly educated head teacher did not know. In fact, the deputy DC did not know, and even worse, the venerable man of God did not either!

**Madam DC:** Of course, your political enemies wrote it. As the chief government official in this district, you have enemies, but you smile with everybody and call it politics. You never listen to anything I say. I have warned you to be careful of Alhaji Brukusu of that no-good party. That man looks at you with an evil twinkle in his left eye, and I pointed this out to you. His wife is a witch. I bet you did not know that man's grandmother was a hunchback. Now that they are writing that 'things are falling apart', you are surprised. Market last Tuesday was the best in months thanks to the new stalls. Because of the gutter you constructed, there has been no flooding this rainy season. In addition, the district recently got a borehole. Is that the way things fall apart? Very soon, the president in faraway Accra will hear that your district is falling apart, all due to your stubbornness in not listening to me. In fact, I have more information I am withholding until an opportune time. The 'rumor-mongerers' will soon be put to utter shame.

The tirade went on for an eternity. The DC, unable to get the wife to pause so he would clarify snuck into the bedroom and within minutes, the bedroom plywood walls were vibrating with his snores. Mental fatigue. That was one of the most eventful days in his tenure as a District Commissioner.

# School Drop-out

Can a schoolboy or girl forget to go to school on a school day? Kojo's absenteeism from school was the talk of the school. He missed school on the flimsiest of excuses: headache, rain, toothache, sunniness, and plain forgetfulness. Another of his foibles was the use of Pidgin English. Pidgin English had been banned in the school because students were losing their ability to construct simple English sentences due to excessive use of this dialect. It interfered with normal English speaking. In pidgin, everything goes. There was nothing like right or wrong. Kojo usually clammed up when teachers were around. He could hardly finish a sentence in English without a couple of pidgin words in it. In standard one, aka 'saa one' in Primary School, our English Language teacher taught us Words and Opposige

The second day when the teacher came for another lesson. He said,

Teacher: Yesterday I taught you Words and their Opposites. Now

what is the opposite of 'GO?

Absolute silence. The teacher was livid. He took out his baranzu and waved it menacingly. To the rescue came Kojo. Kojo hardly came to school. In fact, he even missed the class the previous day. Therefore, it was a wonder that he knew anything about the topic. Oh well...

All the pupils were focused on Kojo the superstar who was going to answer the question and assuage the teacher's anger...

The teacher then roared,

**Teacher:** So, it was only Kojo that I taught yesterday?

You are all dunces! Kojo, come out.

Kojo sprang up and quickly went forward towards the teacher.

**Teacher:** Before you answer, take this cane, and give each one of these nincompoops two strokes. Nincompoop was a new one. Usually he used dunce, stupid or fool to describe people that fit that bill. The children surmised that the teacher's anger was a notch higher. Thanks to the superhero, who never attended class but knew what they did not know, they were going to get only two strokes instead of God knows how many. Two strokes each for 45 pupils! Excitedly, Kojo picked up the baranzu and went to work. Whack! Whack; Whack! Whack! Those who had of-

fended Kojo, which is really most of the class, took stronger strokes. Abu who had refused to give him some of his 'koose and groundnut' at lunchtime took the hardest strokes! So was Makosa who had defied Kojo when he asked for his football for play during recreation break. Kojo gave him a third stroke before the teacher asked him to move on.

By the time he was through, the modern-day Huck Finn was sweating profusely while most of his classmates were wailing uncontrollably. Then the teacher said,

**Teacher:** Keep quiet and listen to your savior. Kojo now tell them the opposite of 'GO'

Kojo raised up his voice, looking askance, and with a stentorian voice, shouted.

**Kojo:** The opposite of GO is "I NO GO GO"

The teacher's eyes nearly popped out of their sockets!

"WHAT!"

Kojo, repeat what you said.

The room was so quiet you could hear a pin drop. The grin on the face of Kojo disappeared. He felt there was something wrong, but he still felt confident in his answer. He had always used pidgin and believed in it more than Webster's dictionary. He spoke

but with less conviction.

**Kojo:** The opposite of GO is "I no go go".

The teacher was doubly infuriated by the fact that Kojo did not know the opposite of the very simplest of words like 'come'; and he was thumbing his nose at the school rules by answering a question in class using the banned pidgin.

**Teacher:** CLASS take the cane and return the favor. Each of you should give the nincompoop two strokes!

Even though he was slow in arithmetic, Kojo speedily did the multiplication of 45 x 2 and got 90. Big trouble! Ninety strokes from a vengeful crowd was too many for him to absorb, especially when he had not adequately padded his buttocks as he usually did. Before anyone could say 'Jack', the artful dodger was out the window...

# Driver's Mate

**D**river's Mate. Kojo had quit school to become an Aplanke aka driver's mate. Which was no news because he had done something as crazy before. Teacher Ponko had sent word that the punishment could be waived. Kojo however didn't believe that his classmates would forgive him. He was sure they would tie him up and lash him, for there was no way a wicked soul like Patapaa would let bygones be bygones. "Vengeance was not for the Lord" when it came to his classmates. Therefore, no amount of exhortation would bring him back. For weeks, no one knew of his whereabouts, until word finally, around that Kojo was an Aplanke aka Driver's mate. As an Aplanke Kojo was the worst nightmare of the passengers on the Bole to Kumasi route. Many people complained to the driver to fire the mate. Unfortunately, the married owner of the vehicle was having an illicit affair with Kojo's niece, which put to bed the reason Konkotibaa the driver could not raise his voice against his saucy Aplanke.

**Mama Abiba:** What is the fare from Bole to Kumasi?

**Kojo:** 50 cedis.

**Mama Abiba:** What? Why so expensive? It used to be c10 when I was a student.

**Kojo:** Madam looking at you that might have been before Ghana attained independence.

**Mama Abiba:** Idiot. I bet you are referring to your mother.

**Mama Abiba:** So, I am to pay c100.00 for this round trip that used to cost less than c20.00 not that long ago!

**Kojo:** Madam the round-trip fare is c130.00.

**Mama Abiba:** Aplanke you should have stayed a little longer in elementary school. You cannot even do simple addition. For your free education, 50 + 50 is 100.

**Kojo:** Madam Thanks for the free SHS, but the return trip costs c80.00. 80+50 = 130.

**Mama Abiba:** How is that possible?

**Kojo:** Madam I am minister for fare collection of this vehicle. It is 130.00. With maximum respect granny it is c130.

**Mama Abiba:** Me granny? Call your master before I curse you.

**Kojo:** You are talking to my master, me.

**Mama Abiba:** I bet you do not have adults in your family. You do

not respect the elderly.

**Kojo:** Yes, to both.

**Mama Abiba:** Do you use a different road or different vehicle when coming back? Does the distance change? How can the fare when going be different from coming back?

**Kojo:** Is the number of days from Monday to Friday the same as Friday to Monday?

**Mama Abiba:** Of course! You can't even count. You need more education.

**Kojo:** Monday, Tuesday, Wednesday, Thursday, Friday makes 5; Friday, Saturday, Sunday, Monday gives you 4. End of story.

# Poisoned Beans

E ven the white-haired and white-goateed erudite Islamic clergy was baffled. How the return journey would cost that much more on the same road, same distance in the same week was most baffling to him. Kojo's sarcastic explanation was always the same. Monday to Friday is not equal to Friday to Monday'. Alhaji was more bemused than angry. Unable to raise the difference in fare, he had reluctantly parted with a quarter bag of the atedua beans he was hauling to Kumasi. Obviously, his profit would reduce but he could make up the difference by increasing his retail prices. Atedua beans was delicacy that was sought after by connoisseurs of good African food. It took longer to cook so it was usually soaked in water overnight. One needed to factor that into consideration if it had to be used for the evening supper. Kojo could not wait to get home to put it on the decrepit kerosene stove because it had been soaked overnight. Just after he finished cooking his bowl of beans, word came from Alhaji Sariki's son advising him to throw away the beans. Rea-

son? The beans had been contaminated with poison. The poison was so powerful that two cows had died after ingesting it, and more than one of the farm workers had been rushed to the local herbalist. Kojo did not believe Alhaji thinking it was a ploy to stop him from enjoying the beans because of how it was obtained. Also, he was not going to throw it away, especially when he had been told that not all the stuff was bad. He had learnt enough from his herbalist uncle, an expert in antidotes, with a collection of concoctions that could get rid of bites by snakes as bad as cobras and mambas. He was aware that a cow is a big animal, and a poison that had killed it must be able to kill a human with ease, but he was not perturbed.  Kojo triple cooked the beans changing the water frequently to make sure all the poison, if any had washed away. Then he gave some to his pet dog Zuma to eat. After waiting a whole hour to see how Zuma fared, he decided the food was safe to eat. The super-soft beans dissolved in the mouth like nothing he had taken in a while. He cursed himself for having taken such a small amount in exchange for the fare, for he could have doubled the fare and Alhaji, under the circumstance would have obliged.

He was about to go to the mango tree to play draught when the gateman came running to tell him that Zuma was dead!

Hey!

No questions asked, Kojo immediately run into the house to try to put in as much antidote for the poison as possible. He downed two bottles of palm oil, chewed 22 bitter kola nuts with 3 long bitter leaf stems. Then he masticated an olonka cupful of walnuts with the shell... no time to crack them. Extra-strength ground Jalapeno Pepper he gobbled in big gulps followed by calash-bash-fuls of stale Pito in a barrel.  Garlic and onions tasted like nectar in his mouth; he devoured them as if it were caviar and washed them down with akpeteshie the local vodka. To him, life on earth was finished! Sweating as if he just emerged from an oven, Kojo managed to get out of the house to catch perhaps his last glimpse of the outside world before succumbing to the poison. He felt very weak; the poison must be too strong for his concoctions of antidote.

There he saw their gateman in the company of a stranger. The man looked very contrite, as if he had done something very wrong and wanted forgiveness or something.

"Amidu is asking for your forgiveness," said Salifu.

Apparently, Amidu was the name of the man in the company of

gateman.

Too terrified to speak lest he hastened his death, Kojo just looked.

"He says he will give you two goats in exchange for the life of the dog."

When Kojo still stood silent, Amidu made it three goats.

Kojo then mustered some strength to ask Salifu what the hell he was talking about.

There Salifu told him that Amidu's truck was the one that had ran over Zuma.

Zuma had not died through poisoning! Which of course meant he Kojo was not going to die after all, hooray.

When Salifu finished speaking, Kojo instead of being angry passionately hugged Amidu as if he were his long-lost brother, and told him to go in peace, no exchange of goat with Zuma. Amidu was shocked. He was just about to up the number of goats thinking Kojo did not respond because the initial offer was too low. From the dog's carcass, Amidu knew Zuma was a fine dog. He asked Kojo, to at least take the two goats. Kojo now back to his senses readily accepted, but Salifu cut in and asked Amidu to maintain the original number of three goats.

As the two began to haggle, Kojo's tummy began to complain

loudly. He just remembered that he had put in a lot of stuff, and this was something that merited his attention. He knew he was going to live, and frankly did not care about goats. The concern now was how to get rid of the antidotes in his body. That was the decade old saga of the poisoned beans, which were not poisoned beans after all.

Kojo was having a hard time in Cape Coast without a doubt. So, it was with great joy that he received word of a visit from Gertrude, his former American chemistry teacher, and her family. That was good news. He had already met the party in Ofinso, and there could not be a better group to rub shoulders with. When the party arrived, they ate in the Savoy, the fanciest restaurant in town, and visited the tourist sites. The Konkonte treks were suspended. With his food woes now over, he began to appreciate even a better Cape Coast. Eventually, the parents left, but Gertrude had fallen in love with Cape Coast and sped back as soon as they were gone. On his visits, she stayed in an apartment in Cape Vars. The two friends spent an awful amount of time at the beach. They tiptoed in the sand or sat with legs outstretched teasing the waves, but mostly they sat and witnessed the battle of attrition between the waves and the land. The waters careened forward,

attacking everything in its path before ebbing slowly away as if spent by the effort of the assault. That was the beauty of the wave; from afar, it looked awesomely terrifying, as it strutted like a male peacock in heat before dissolving in a tranquil and disarming manner at the shore, not unlike the limpness of the male body after an orgasmic frenzy. It is an enthralling spectacle to witness this much ado about nothing sequence as it tossed and turned in its endless march to subdue or be subdued by the land. It looked dangerous, but it was beautiful—a primordial, natural, pristine, and hypnotic type of beauty. Teacher and student wandered around until they found a log. On this log did the pair sit, holding hands and leaning on each other for warmth as they witnessed the timeless combat between the infinite ocean and the endless earth, which simply reduces to a love affair between water and land. In this culture, people did not hold hands as an expression of love, and the incongruous spectacle of a young black man holding hands with a buxom white lady would have caused a minor commotion. Therefore, during the day, they walked with the proper and decent separation between the two, the lady in the wake of the man. Earlier in the day, the market women had serenaded him for getting such a full woman as a consort. He had had to explain that that was not the case at all; they were friends, and there was nothing more to it. It was when they further learned that she was his ex-teacher that they were able to understand the nature of the relationship. With an ample behind, nice waist, supple neck, adequate-sized legs, and topped over with a beautiful and authentic smile, a smile that could melt any heart that the blue eyes fixated on, Gertrude to them was an authentic African beauty with a white skin. Gertrude's infectious smile mirrored the mom. The Allison family had visited Ghana the previous summer. The dad, a big strapping Santa Claus, was a medical officer with a practice, somewhere in Mississippi. Dr. Allison was a teddy bear whose very look cried for a hug. The mother was also very bubbly and affectionate. The kids were overly excited by their first Africa trip until they saw their first lizard. That was one thing worth remembering about them, their utter terror of lizards. For the first few days, they stayed indoors under lock and key because of the little creatures. In most African villages, lizards outnumbered people by a ratio of ten to one. Thus, trying to stay away from these ubiquitous, fierce-looking crocodilian imitations was a lost cause.

It was when these white boys trembled on the sighting of these respectful creatures that Kojo began to have some empathy. For on closer look lizards are miniature crocodiles really, and crocodiles are not teddy bears. The irony is that there is not an animal God created that is less harmful and more cowardly than the lizard. It took days of coaxing and cajoling before the boys ventured out.

# The Game of Tele-Tele

For weeks, the favorite night pastime of the kids that congregated under the Baobab in Sakasaka was 'Tele-Tele'. This was a 'Cops and Robbers' game where the boys acted the part of robbers with distinction. However, the receptionists who were the police or good guys, were not that good. The game went thus: one of the boys would enter the telephone booth, pick up the handset and would be automatically connected with a telephone receptionist. The receptionist would then ask the customer what telephone number he or she wanted to connect to. This short interlude was free.

The kid in the booth would indulge in a fantasy that could take any form depending on the kid, whilst the rest of the group acted as lookouts. For the precious first minutes, this conversation would go on until a suspicious adult was spotted or a paying customer showed up. They would all run to congregate at another of the many telephone booths scattered around the city. There they would interview the boy that went inside the last booth and find out what was said.

Animal Mimicry: Kofi had a gift of perfect animal mimicry. After entering the booth, he barked like a dog. The bark was so authentic and so loud that the lady almost dropped the headset. It was only after she perceived some voices laughing at the other end that she calmed down. Kofi then meowed like a cat, mooed like a cow, and squealed like a pig before they ran away to congregate under their baobab auditorium. They moved to a different booth and repeated the game, but now with a different kid in the booth.

**Young Mallam:** Soko, whose father was a Mallam asked to pray for the receptionist, so she could be exorcised of her witchcraft, claiming to be a wizard himself. He told her that he was going to invite her into a group of which he was a member, claiming how much fun it was to fly around on a broomstick and party all night. When questioned what drink they used at the parties, Soko said it was COCA COLA instead of blood that the other witches' groups used. Laughter could be heard from the receptionist's office even outside the booth.

**Fart Expert:** TM was an expert in farting. The one chance he got to go into the booth, he made such a loud sound with his mouth that the receptionist dropped the headset and rushed out holding her nose before bursting out laughing. She thought she was

going to start smelling something odious before she realized the folly of the whole thing.

The boys thought it was funny, but they were serious distractions that tied up personnel that were already stretched for time. After enduring the spate of distractions from the anonymous juvenile delinquents, the telephone operators plotted revenge, and the sport took on an ominous tone. Police officers were speedily dispatched to locations where those prank calls came from. The response times of the police were however slow because they came on foot. Patrol cars if any were for matters that are more serious. The female operators countered these slow responses by enticing the callers into longer conversations. They prolonged the dialogues by using titillating language to buy time for the cops. Even near misses by the police did not stop these wretched boys from pursuing this dangerous past time. Jato lost his singlet in one these near misses, which was no big deal because the tattered singlet was ready for retirement.

**Young President:** After a long lull, it was time for them to indulge their dangerous pastime with the police. Kojo was the next to go to the booth. The president's popular Independence speech had been heard on radio numerous times. Most adults knew the

first line and perhaps the last line. Children, however, didn't care a hoot; to them that was adult stuff. Kojo however loved it, and usually regurgitated the speech to the annoyance and amazement of his playmates. In fact, they didn't know whether the words and sentences were accurate, but certain keywords in the speech made them to believe that Kojo could be right. He told his friends that he would give the speech to the next receptionist when it reached his turn. And soon enough it was his turn.

"At long last, the battle has ended! And thus, Ghana, your beloved country is free forever!

And yet again, I want to take the opportunity to thank the people of this country; the youth, the farmers, the women who have so nobly fought and won the battle.

Also, I want to thank the valiant ex-service men who have so co-operated with me in this mighty task of freeing our country from foreign rule and imperialism.

And, as I pointed out... from now on, today, we must change our attitudes and our minds. We must realize that from now on we are no longer a colonial but free and independent people. But also, as I pointed out, that also entails hard work. That new Africa is ready to fight his own battles and show that after all the black

man can manage his own affairs.

We are going to demonstrate to the world, to the other nations, hat we are prepared to lay our foundation – our own African personality.

As I said to the Assembly a few minutes ago, I made a point that we are going to create our own Africa personality and identity. It is the only way we can show the world that we are ready for our own battles.

But today, may I call upon you all, that on this great day let us all remember that nothing can be done unless it has the purpose and support of God.

We have won the battle and again rededicate ourselves ... OUR INDEPENDENCE IS MEANINGLESS UNLESS IT IS LINKED UP WITH THE TOTAL LIBERATION OF AFRICA."

The click alerted the spellbound receptionist that the speech by the little man at the other end was over. But for the voice, she would have even thought that the president himself had pranked her on the phone. For days, Habiba continued to gush to other receptionists about the speech by one of the pests that had been tormenting them the past few weeks.

The P&T operators irritated by these phone pranks castigated the

police for their ineptness in stopping the little rascals. Important calls were left unattended because they spent precious minutes before realizing that these were prank calls. The police resolved to put an end to this nuisance by doubling the number of cops on the beat.

**The Beggar:** Toko was from an extremely poor home, and this was reflected in the way he dressed. For starters, he sometimes wore his school uniform to church on Sundays. Due to the hot and humid weather, most of the kids were sometimes bare chested, except that Toko was always bare chested; unless you consider the tattered singlet that barely covered his upper torso as an apparel. Toko had engaged the receptionist in a longer conversation and had vented to her about his circumstances. The lady that had suffered so much abuses from these urchins saw this as an opportunity to final meet one of her nocturnal adversaries. She promised to help him if he could visit her during working hours. Toko, salivating on meeting a rich person to help ameliorate his circumstances took the woman on her word. So, there stood the devil of the night. The symbol of the torments that the receptionists had endured for weeks stood resplendent in a dirty school uniform, so tattered that his butt showed. Aisha was even

moved. She was expecting a hateful little vagrant, but this frail and melancholic character was someone she couldn't turn over to the police. Alas, that was now beyond her control. The security people, who were expecting him, took one look and grabbed him by the collar. The beatings commenced even as they dragged him to his house, where the second set of beatings from his parents would continue.

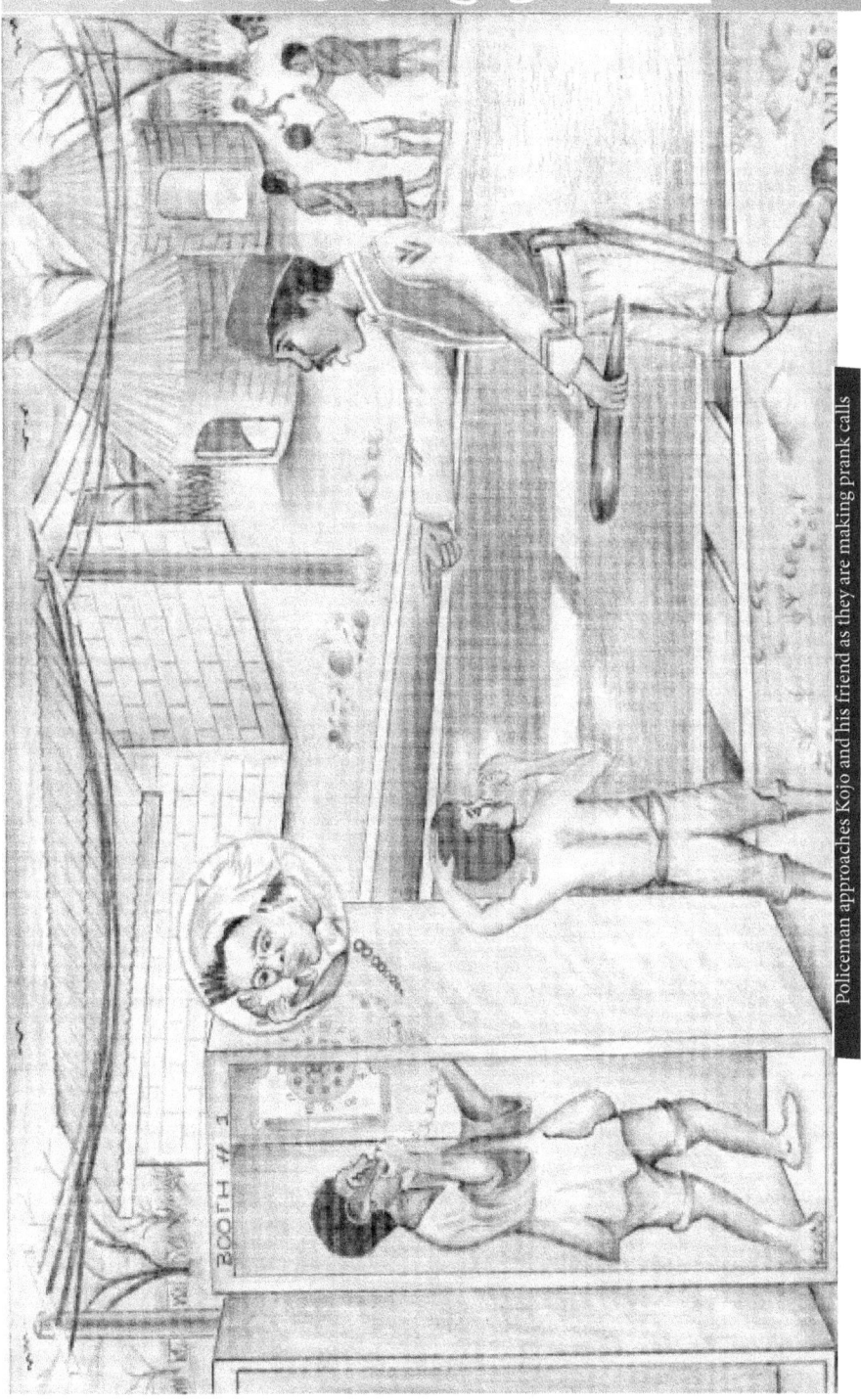

Policeman approaches Kojo and his friend as they are making prank calls

# The Foot Breaker Game

**G**ame on. Saturday mornings are for nothing else but kicking leather so to speak. From nowhere, Kojo had conjured up a round object that seemed exactly like a regular-sized leather football. This Saturday morning Sala had run into Kojo as he was bouncing this strange object up and down whilst clutching a regular-looking one in the other hand. The challenge to kick a ball past a marker was issued forth. Kicking a ball past a marker was the way the weekend football games started. Kojo issued this challenge with a wicked twinkle in his eye that should have alerted Sala to some trickery, for this modern day Kwaku Ananse was always plotting new intrigues. Moving back a couple of steps, Sala administered a gentle kick. Almost immediately, he reached for his foot in agony. Glancing in Kojo's direction, he saw the trickster rolling on the ground convulsed with laughter and farting to boot. Alas! Sala had discovered to his chagrin that the spherical ball was not made of leather, rubber, or plastic; rather it felt like steel, concrete or lead or something of a very dense nature. Engulfed in pain and livid with rage, Sala

attempted to lunge at Kojo but went sprawling on the ground for he could not put any weight on the injured leg. His pain turned into anger and then to embarrassment at having been so easily deceived. As the pain subsided, his machismo took over and he joined in the laughter telling Kojo how soft the ball was. However, Kojo was not buying.

Sala: The initial facial contortion was only a pretense; it was nothing really.

Kojo: Liar, you were crying for your granddaddy.

They were in the middle of this exchange when the first of a stream of victims showed up. Sala went to Kojo's corner in challenging Musa to kick the ball past that marker, and soon enough the newbie was easing back to swallow the bait.

The scenario was the same; in a couple of seconds Musa was furiously massaging his foot to ease the pain, then getting ticked off on discovering the trickery, then in a show of braggadocio pretending it did not hurt, and finally assisting in luring the next victim. After the fifth victim, Kojo decided to charge a fee for the privilege of participating in the sport! Anyone attempting to kick the object was to pay a penny. Others that had undergone that ordeal and wanted to visit the same embarrassment

Boys playing the Foot breaker Game

on their friends lured many of the new players. Later, the consummate businessperson and entrepreneur extraordinaire made the terms even more generous; those that could not afford the cash payment could pay in kind; eggs, marble, the local pastries amaasa and koose, or something valuable. There were scores of wild guinea fowl in the surrounding areas. These birds lived close to human habitations, and laid their eggs in shrubs and thickets, which could be collected by anyone willing to go drive off the mother hen. The mother hen usually put up a no contest fight. By nightfall, Kojo was the richest boy in town. Among his loot for a day of dishonest labor were farthings, halfpennies, pennies, marbles, guinea fowl eggs, koosé, amaasa and even kola-nuts. Everyone else had a bruise on the leg. So, like the walking wounded of a defeated platoon straight out of the battlefield, the participants in Kojo's newest intrigue, the Foot Breaker Challenge, limped towards their various homes.

# The Excuse

Helpless was the appropriate description of the children. Like the remnants of a defeated army, they slowly trudged home. Most had to miss school and it was not long before the architect of these crimes was fingered out. The Baobab boys as they were sometimes referred to, had repeatedly been warned to stay away from him, which was a difficult task because prescient and ubiquitous Kojo seemed to pop up where and when least expected. He even showed up in church during rollcall for church attendance. Taking rollcall was random and the results communicated to Sakasaka Primary school. Pu¬pils that made it to church on rollcall days were cited for special mention, because it was assumed that they went to church regularly. Kojo's sense of prescience made it seem as if he had inside information on this especially important event. The few days he went to church, the Sunday school teacher, a

Father Lazarus speedily leaving Sunday School classroom after Kojo fouled air

Roman Catholic priest from Spain had his hands full, and then some. Father Juan had disappeared for months. Rumors of his death were rife, and it was a pleasant surprise when this good man showed up in church one Sunday and proclaimed to have been healed by God. Skinny and pale, Father Juan looked as if he had risen from the dead and was promptly nicknamed Juan by Kojo. The long-suffering Man of God did not mind at all when the name was used in his hearing; proclaiming it was a testimony of his hardiness, resilience and of course the Lord's favor.

Anytime Kojo showed up for Sunday school, he turned the place into a concert party. He would imitate animal sounds, whistle, dive under tables, make faces when the father's back was turned, and then ask the silliest questions. A most annoying habit was his penchant for going out of the class on the flimsiest of reasons. A condition for going out was to ask permission. Kojo dramatized the permission-asking process to the point where the father wished he would not have to obey that cardinal rule. For example, he would ask permission to go use the urinal, attend nature's call, to cough, to spit, sneeze and even to clear his throat. The Catholic father was especially befuddled by the fact that the little demon would ask to use the urinal five minutes after returning

from the toilet. One Sunday, Kojo was at his mischievous worst to the point where the long-suffering priest could not take it anymore. The children were astonished to witness a white man turn into a red man before their very eyes. They quieted down and for the next few minutes, the room was silent. Juan forbade

anyone from stepping outside until the session was over. Kojo was impressed but not cowed. Soon enough his hand shot up again and he started making his way towards Juan.

Juan asked him what it was this time, but the boy did not respond until he was standing next to him, and then came up with the ultimate excuse; he wanted to go outside to pass gas! The man of God was not falling for any of the little heathen's tricks any longer. He believed it was a ploy to go out again and dared him. "You can do that dirty thing right here!" yelled Juan. The room was deathly quiet when Kojo let go of a deep, rumbling, primal sound not unlike a distant earthquake from the very bowels of the earth. Father Juan stood frozen. The emaciated Catholic father looked like he would drop off the precipice of life if a breeze but nudged a little. However, moments later he was sprinting outside with a handkerchief over the nose, and with the children screaming with glee.

# The Feast of Leftovers

nstead of playing 'gutter-gutter', 'hide and seek', incessant Samson-Hercules make-believe battles' and generally being a kid, Sala was cooped up with his grandpa preparing for a court battle. Now the court case was over. They lost, but it was over. To say that Sala missed Kojo was an understatement. And he dearly wanted to make up for lost time. They agreed to pool resources together to go eat at the exclusive Hajia's 'Don't Mind Your Wife' Chop Bar, the best TZ eatery in town.TZ was the acronym for the popular "Tuo Zafi" dish and Hajia Hasetu popularly known, as Hajia was the proprietress of the best TZ eating spot in the universe. That joint was mostly for adults that could afford to spend hard cash. Hajia's place was organized along the lines of a regular African self-service eatery. One had to join a "First-in-First-out" or FIFO queue, buy the stuff and choose their table. On Sundays, service time in the FIFO queue could get long because Hajia was

the sole person that dispensed of the stuff. While in the queue the boys heard the amounts of money being bandied about and quickly realized that, even with the accumulated pennies, Hajia's was out of their league. A dish of TZ comprises specially pre-pared balls of corn dough, soup, and meat. Out of these three, the dough and the meat had to be paid for separately; the soup was free. The dough was not expensive, but TZ is almost never eaten without meat; and the two musketeers found to their cha-grin that they could afford the balls but not the meat. Too late to back out, they got the TZ without meat amidst mocking from the adults around them. Hajia kindly added free bone fragments to the soup triggering even more laughter.  The boys settled in an unobtrusive corner and commenced meting out justice to the TZ. The adults were having a good time. Most ate in groups of threes and fours, in big bowls of TZ with enough meat to make the dough invisible. The boys felt out of place, especially with the cigarette smoke. Kojo was eating slowly and taking in the scene. Meanwhile Sala furiously ate, oblivious to the surroundings. Sud-denly, Kojo grabbed the hand of his friend and made an interest-

ing remark.

'We should not have bought the food at all.'

Looking around him for the first time, Sala understood what that meant. Many of the tables had meals eaten to various fractions of completion. Some were half-eaten, third eaten, quarter-eaten, and hardly touched at all. A lot of surplus aka sipolo, some with big chunks of meat that they could never afford otherwise, were at their mercy. The challenge was to determine when a customer was done. That was not too difficult. If the water in the washbasin was used, it meant the customer was done. The partly eaten food was to be thrown away and the table wiped clean for the next customer. If the water was clean then the customer had probably left for a quick dash to the washroom, or to get more salt. There was a big stigma attached to eating leftovers at anywhere but home, and the boys knew they would be teased to death if other kids found out about their newest tantalizing adventure. On the other hand, if this could be pulled off then there was going to be an inexhaustible supply of TZ meals till kingdom come. They had to proceed with caution, but they were going for it. Their new modus operandi was simple: Join the queue, buy a small piece of TZ sans meat, enter into the eating room, very slowly eat the portion, identify a table with sipolo, switch your table with sipolo table, and help oneself.

Nanka and friend at the Feast of Leftovers

On this first day, the boys had walked through the front door and bought their own stuff forestalling any ideas that they were sipolo eaters. This appeared to be the best approach. The customers had been classified into two; a dead customer was one that was done, never to come back; a live customer was one that was not done.

Customers did take breaks for one reason or the other. The taste of the soup might not meet the liking of a customer, and he would make a beeline to the soup cage and collect a little salt. The woman serving the soup would then point to the salt bowl, and the customer would dip the thumb and two other fingers, grab some crystals of salt and head back to their meals. The crafty kids had also observed that, to prevent the salt crystals from falling from the fingers, the customers always inverted the hands after dipping into the salt bowl so that the palm was facing upward. Anytime one could observe a figure with inverted fingers with the palm open upwards, it meant he was carrying salt, and was on his way back to continue from where he left off. The dilemma of switching a sipolo table was twofold; to wait too long meant they lost to the bar help; to move too early risked taking the food of a live customer. To their pleasant surprise, there was so much

sipolo that it was not necessary to buy any TZ. However, it was the "bought TZ" that granted them access to the inner sanctum from where they could feast on the sipolo. Other Children their age had not yet discovered this brilliant idea, so they had no challengers. Therefore, for the next few weeks the two obnoxious but clever boys dined with Tamale's crème de la crème at minimal cost.

One inauspicious Sunday, they went through the regular routine and confidently sat down to await sipolo. Adjacent to them was a man in flowing jambalaya eating alone. It was always a good omen when they ate alone for diners are less likely to leave any leftovers if they are in a group. In front of their newest neighbor sat a huge bowl with enough pieces of meat to recreate a full-size goat. The man did look the wealthy type. Kojo was mentally calculating how much the dish was worth when the man dipped his hand in the washbasin and left the canteen. Normally they waited long enough to make sure the customer had really left before they pronounced judgment on a dish as sipolo. However, they did not want to lose this good-looking booty to their main competition, the bar helps. The bar helps had gotten to know of the operations of the two boys and bore them legitimate resentment. The two

rascals were getting to be regulars at this eatery, which was not possible because, based on the clothes they wore they should not be able to afford eating there at all. Fact is the boys stuck out like a sore thumb, for the patrons were mostly adults who had money to burn. Even the smoky interior due to the many smokers among the clientele made it a must-avoid place for children. Secondly, the two boys kept too long in the canteen, and this long-wait prevented patrons who could splurge from getting seated early. The bar helps knew they were being robbed of the sipolo that they usually could take home to members of the family. The boys also sensed the animosity. They knew they dared not touch any sipolo in the presence of the bar helps, and always waited for them to make their exit before effecting any table switching.

Not long after this rich-looking man had washed his hands and left, Kojo pronounced him "dead" and switched tables. They were busily doing justice to the meal when they observed a man in the distance making his way towards them. Since there was no hand inversion, they assumed it was a new arrival, perhaps on his way to join the queue. It was only when he was almost on top of them that they realized it was the man that sat adjacent to them. Obviously, he was still "alive". Their vaunted "dead or alive" iden-

tification system had failed.

There was no escape from this situation. Curses and insults were flying left and right. The man had a voice to match his frame. Obviously famished, he had not invested so much in his meal for nothing. He invoked the curses of both God and the devil on the little miscreants. The bar help were the most excited and might have caused bodily harm but for Hajia's intervention. They threw their adversaries out with as much commotion as possible. With their tails between their legs, the boys made for the exit even as voices continued to rain insults on them. That epitome of ignominy signaled the end of their sipolo days in Hajia's joint.

# Oversized Coat

J ust as was expected, Kojo was in trouble. After break-
ing the foot of his friends in the Foot Breaker game,
the brush with the law during the Tele-tele games, the
scene he made at Hajia's "Don't Mind Your Wife" TZ eatery and
his shameful behavior in sending the venerable Cath¬olic father
scurrying from Sunday school, Kojo was in big trouble. The uncle had had it. He was now shipping the little boy off. Kojo was
on his way to another uncle in a quaint little town somewhere
in the bowels of the country. The eight-year-old boy cut some
spectacle in his travel paraphernalia. He was dressed in an oversized old coat that hugged the knees, a faded undershirt, and a
pair of faded khaki shorts. A large straw hat swallowed the head
giving the appearance that it was meant to hide than protect the
head from the sun.The coat was heavy, and he sweated in the
sweltering Harmattan sun. And to cap it all, he was also "driving
a shit truck", local parlance for walking barefoot. The first set of
people he met glanced in his direction and broke into laughter.
Having no idea why those people were so rude, he decided not

to ask them for directions. When everybody that saw him in his full regalia broke into laughter the boy realized he had no choice but to ask anyhow and headed for a small group in a hut. The people at the palm wine parlor were amazed when they found out that the comedic-looking little stranger was related to "Master", the well-respected head teacher at the middle school. Even more amazing was the resemblance between the two. They quit laughing and the proprietor personally escorted him to his father.

Kojo was surprised at his reception. In Tamale he was a trend setter, but these fashion-challenged village folks looked at him with derision. The uncle took one look at his nephew and wished he could disown the boy. And that was the end of Kojo's life as a Tamalean, a resident of the great city of Tamale.

Kojo, sweating in oversized coat arrives at new town

# An Ode to a Little Town

**K**umasi-Kumasi-Kumasi hollered the Aplanke as he gesticulated towards the people standing by the roadside waiting for a lorry to transport them to the big city. Pokukrom was small even by small town standards. The town was bisected by the trunk road that linked the city of Kumasi with Bechem in the Brong- Ahafo region. On one side of the town were the market stalls where pet¬ty traders mobbed the vehicles and hawked eat-on-the-go food items. Bofrot, Sweet bun, corn- on-the-cob, and all sorts of snack were dispensed at a small fee, to the travel weary that paused here on their way to the deeper hinterland. And on the opposite and far bigger side were the majority of homes of the residents many of whom had relocated from the old Pokukrom, a few miles off the trunk road. In effect, this Pokukrom was a new township. The sections were very unequal giving the impression that a workman with a defective compass had done the bisection. Regularly rumbling through

the little town were monster trucks that hauled timber logs from afar. The trucks were nicknamed Mimbuo, meaning "the rocks of Mim" because they generally originated from the timber town of Mim further up north.

Pokukrom was surrounded by the forest and with it the dangers and profits of the forest. The forest was a very generous neighbor; from it was found delicacies such as snails, mushroom and nkontomire. When snails were in season, it was a matter of stepping yards into the bush to pick them up. Mushrooms were also in abundance, but some caution ought to be exercised for some were reputed to be poisonous; plucking them was an art. From the adjoining cottages and villages, farmers inundated the little town with plantain, cocoyam, local yam, and all manner of food crops, which they sold at rock bottom prices. Living in this blessed environ did not require too much hard cash.

During the first few weeks, the red carpet was rolled for the new arrival from the great city of the north. Unlike kids his age, he didn't have to go to the adjoining farms to carry foodstuffs and firewood and best of all to the stream to fetch water. There was no pipe borne water and the stream that supplied the town with water was a good distance away. In the early mornings children

had to make multiple trips to the stream with buckets and gallons balanced on their heads filled with water. That was a chore he disdained and made him pine for Tamale. Luckily, he was exempt from that, for now.

His uncle made a lot of fuss about how lean and bony he was and put him on a crash diet to fatten him up, but gave up when he realized the boy wasn't putting on any pounds even though he was eating like a pig; apparently, he was one of those hyperactive kids that could eat a horse and not show it because their metabolism rate was in the stratosphere. The uncle in Tamale had said something like he roamed as if "he had eaten a dog's hind leg", the idiom for a vagabond or anyone that roamed so unceasingly. One weekend, there was a competitive soccer match between Pokukrom and Mankranso, a much bigger town in the same district. The venue was the soccer field of the local primary school. The match was well attended with spectators three or four deep standing around the edges of the playing field. The little boy managed to wriggle his way to the edge of the playing field closest to the field of play. Suddenly, an errant powerful shot went in his direction, hit his leg, lifted him off the ground, and deposited him on his butt, throwing the whole arena into laughter. People couldn't

believe that a soccer ball could lift someone off the ground that high. The little man bounced up and skipped a couple of times to let everyone, who was watching the game know he wasn't hurt and beat a retreat through the forest of legs away from the edge of the park. That was an indication of how light he was.

His Tamale accoutrements that threw bystanders into fits of laughter were thrown away and replaced with a new wardrobe. He also received a new set of toiletries. The coolest part was the toothbrush. He brushed his teeth many times a day standing outside the house so the whole world could see him. Every boy used a chewing stick or plantain fibers with ash, so it was a spectacle of some sorts as he went through the motions of cleaning his teeth. Kids used to walk past where he stood to see for themselves if the story making the rounds that the new kid on the block used a toothbrush was true. Truth be told, the toothbrush was a contraption he didn't particularly like; unlike a chewing stick you couldn't jettison it as soon as you were done with it. Most times he found himself chewing the brush like a chewing stick and it did look beat up after less than a week of use. He brushed the teeth so frequently that he went through a tube of toothpaste in a week and that was it for the uncle. But to impress his peers he

still did a lot of brushing; soap, ash and anything that could foam were used until the novelty wore off. After that he gladly went back to chewing stick and was able to participate in the popular sport of "who can spit farthest".

There were a lot of myths about the north that tended to both romanticize and vilify that part of the country. The north was spoken of with awe. Kids flocked to him to ascertain the truth of these stories and he did his best to answer the questions, but not without some major embellishment. How he wished Kojo was in his position; he would have painted a picture that might have called for his coronation as king of this little town. Kojo could have made good money answering dumb question after dumb question. Preposterous stories of lions, elephants, hyenas, and other wild animals roaming in the streets had gained currency, and he was not the one to debunk them and reduce his standing in their eyes. He told people about imaginary encounters with wild beasts. But for some reason he never broached the close shave with the crocodile. That incident still terrified him, and he couldn't bring himself to demystify it by recounting it. For some weird reason he thought the encounter was a sacred one and wanted it to be treated as such.

Pokukrom was depressingly small. As the popular kid cliché went, it was so small that a person with enough water in the system could pee around it if he set his mind to it. "Krom" meant town in the vernacular, so Pokukrom meant Poku's town. The little town was named after a man called Poku who might have been the founder, or the first prominent person to settle there. It was a far cry from the pulsating metropolis of Tamale where a kid could roam for hours and a newbie could even get lost. For a city boy, Mensa did not find the forest and bushes appealing. According to Kojo, forests were the abode of dangerous animals such as snakes, hyenas, and lions; forests were also the haunts of vampires, dragons, leprechauns and beings that were created by God for only one purpose, to terrify.

Hardly a day passed without the alarm "owo o" to alert upon the sighting of a snake somewhere in the neighborhood. Snakes were weird and loathsome and were avoided like the plague. As a result, they were pursued relentlessly and their headless carcasses littered compounds. Dead snakes without the heads cut off were known to strike out, especially if stepped upon. As the saying went, "the only way to ensure a snake is really dead is to cut off the head".

The other residents of the forest were a bigger worry. Unlike snakes they were invisible, so he was told, and unlike snakes nobody pursued dragons and leprechauns. According to those in the know, leprechauns were dwarfs that looked like little humans, but with their feet turned in the opposite direction so that judging by their footprints one could not tell whether they were going north or south. It appeared that all they did was beat up on people that crossed them, a task accomplished easily since they could choose to be invisible. Mainly they responded to coded incantations by magicians, such as Professor Hindu. This famed magician was said to command an army of the little beings, which he could unleash on a little town if the town incurred his ire. He could also conjure gifts, money, and other goodies to people in a town that rolled the welcome mat. Stories, from far and wide, talked of the prowess of this magician. Kojo claimed to have witnessed a performance of this pseudo Hindu and seen some great magic. The kids of Pokukrom were no less enamored of this venerable professor and aspired to be like him, by following in his footsteps.

# THE
# MIDDLE SCHOOL
# YEARS

# Ananse the Zookeeper

L ying came easily to Kwaku Ananse. Now he was broke. After many weeks of deep thought, Ananse came up with an idea. Hurriedly, he went to Kontromfi the moneylender and tried to borrow some money to start a business. Because of his reputation, Kontromfi was not accommodating at all, but eventually, he gave half of the requested amount to Ananse, who used it to start a zoo. On opening day, Ananse set the entrance fee at C10.00. No one showed up. The next day, he reduced it to c5.00. Still, no success.Ananse then reduced the fee to c1.00, and still people did not come. One weekend, he made the entry fee zero. When the announcement came out, people came from far and near to enjoy Ananse's magnanimity. Soon enough the zoo was filled with a queue outside. Among the people lucky enough to get in early was Kontromfi. Ananse quietly locked the gate of the zoo, and then set the lions free. There was a stampede to the exit. Kontromfi begged to be let out. Even as they talked, the hungry lions roared outside trying to get to where the two were haggling. Ananse brought out the loan documents and asked him to sign that the loan was forgiven. The moneylender hurriedly obliged, and quickly hightailed it out of the zoo. Ananse then set the exit fee at C100.00. Those with enough money fought for the right to pay and exit. Those without money borrowed from friends and family. Others borrowed from Ananse, who had by now become a loan shark. He set his loan rate at the highest and asked for property as collateral.

After this terrifying incident, people kept a respectable distance from Ananse's zoo. The zoo thus faced closure and the animals started dying off. That is until Kwaku Ananse came out with another idea.

Ananse told the chief of the town that the town must feed his lions because they brought tourists to the town. The chief flatly refused. One Saturday, Ananse released the lions into the town. He told the chief that until he was given 3 cows to feed the hungry lions, he was not going to lock them up. The whole Saturday, nobody in the little town ventured out. The dogs, cats, goats, sheep, chickens all stayed indoors. Even the ubiquitous lizards were scarce. Finally, the chief gave in and three cows were offered to Ananse, who promptly slaughtered one to feed the li-

ons, kept one and sold one to the town butcher. Ananse pulled the same stunt the following weekend. People in the town were terrified of Ananse. In fact, Ananse was more powerful and richer than the chief. Ntikuma Ananse's first son heard that his father had turned into a terror. Knowing how cowardly his father was, Ntikuma did not believe it. Ananse cavorting with lions was something he could never bring himself to believe. That is, unless these were a special breed of lions. Ntikuma thus began investigations. That was when he found out that the lions were cast offs from a circus. The animals were defanged and were not capable of catching even a chicken.

Armed with this information, Ntikuma came to town and confronted his father. With his secret blown, Ananse left town to avoid the wrath of the townspeople, whom he had intimidated and robbed for many months.

# The Bush Orchestra

**M**orning dew is wet, after all it is water, and Kojo did not like water on his skin. But it was therapeutic. That was what drove him to the bushes regularly to commune with nature. With abundant rainfall, fertile land and the strong work ethic of the indigenous folk, food was in abundance. The times when he would feel a little hungry, Kojo would go deep into the bushes where fruits in various stages of ripening were at his behest. Pawpaw, bananas, man¬goes, avocado, oranges, and guava were there begging to be plucked. Wherever there are fruits there are birds. Birds of all shapes, sizes, and feathers fluttered far and near. In his reconnaissance trips to explore the new town, he had chanced upon a fascinating fruit tree with a branch that was almost perpendicular to the main trunk. The transplanted city boy used to sit on this branch and watch entranced as birds of disparate plumages stopped by to feed and sing. According to Kojo, one day he placed a piece of fruit in his palm, which was ignored by the birds. After many

Kojo at the Jungle Bird Orchestra

attempts, one little bird hopped and snatched the fruit. Mesmerized, he slipped, fell, and landed in the shrubs below. The next few days he did the same thing and failed to lure a bird. Nevertheless, he discovered that the birds were not as easily frightened off when he got closer. Finally, another bird snatched the fruit but did not fly off. It just pecked and ate off his palm. He was beyond exhilaration. With time, the birds did not flinch even when he was near. Perhaps, as a rule, the birds always sang after feeding before they flew away. Maybe they were saying goodbye to the other birds, or thanking God for a wonderful meal, who knows. Going to the tree to exclusively listen and watch the birds feeding and singing became his number one pastime. Informing his friends was out of the question. His village friends sometimes skipped school to go bird hunting with their catapults. If they ever found out about the tree, that would be the end of his St. Francis of Assisi days. As obnoxious as he was, Kojo was so persuasive he could charm a bird out of a tree. Literally. Nobody ever witnessed any of the scenes he described, but this was the story he stuck to. The birds did not sing the same song all the time. They varied the song perhaps based on their moods or perhaps the sweetness of the fruit or perhaps the company

they had. To his mild surprise, the smaller birds did not necessarily have the smallest voices. Nevertheless, the little birds had
soprano and alto voices, whilst the bigger birds had the tenors
and the occasional baritone. Sometimes for instances, there were
so many birds of exquisite colors on a branch that from afar, it
appeared the tree had sprouted diamonds, rubies, and topaz in
place of leaves. The kaleidoscope of changing colors as new sets
of birds arrived was an extraordinary sight. With the abundance
of so much fruit, the birds did sing their hearts out as:

*The cooing of the Cuckoo,*

*The hooting of the night Owl,*

*The grating of the Sparrow,*

*The chirping of the Nightingale,*

*The yodeling of the Robin,*

*The whistling of the Heron,*

*The tweeting of the Cardinal,*

*The hooing of the Dove,*

*The pecking of the Woodpecker, and*

*the swooshing of the Canary*

combined into a blend that could put the Vienna Philharmonic orchestra to shame. It was like nectar to the ears. Perhaps Adam and Eve were not bored in the Garden of Eden. Surrounded by so much beauty and sweetness Kojo reflected on how wondrous life was even in the interminable lethargy of a small village, where the days merged into each other without any excitement worthy of note. The longing for Tamale, with its frenetic pace was now at the periphery of his thinking.

# The Teacher from Hell

Nativity plays for the Easter season was an annual event in some schools and Churches in the country. Pokukrom LA primari school organized this event that regularly required help in the form of palm branches from the pupils. It was a struggle for the little ones to cut down the palm fronds. Opanin Tutu's cutlass made mincemeat of the branches and within a few minutes, Kojo had more than enough to cover his allotment. He was sad to see the branches fall off for he was really enjoying their slow waltz as they swayed back and forth. According to Rev. Nyamékyé aka "God's gift", in his sermon the previous Sunday, palm branches were used to welcome Jesus to Jerusalem. These same branches were the favorite haunts of snakes, how ironic.With the branches tied and set on his head, Kojo began the short walk to school. There was going to be a plentiful supply of palm fronds for a great Easter Nativity.

Classes were in session when he got to the school compound. From afar, he could hear the booming voice of teacher Kunta. He froze. Teacher Kunta was a balding, stocky, bow-legged, heavily

built man with a mean scowl that sent shivers down the spine. Kids went in the opposite direction once they beheld his menacing figure heading their way. Kojo particularly went to great lengths to avoid passing by his house even after school. Teacher Kunta's Class 1 was the first classroom encountered as one made his way from the direction of town, from whence he was coming. To go to his classroom in primary five, he had to go past class 1. The school building sat on an inclined elevation. Stairs the height of a child were used to access the building at the class 1 end.

Wicked teacher Kunte lashing Nanka

At this end, one could crouch beside the stairs and not be visible from the classroom. Terrified of the prospect of being seen, Kojo crouched and tried to tiptoe his way up. Unfortunately, the rustling palm fronds made enough noise to alert Teacher Kunta, and he came around to investigate. There, he found a little boy in a crouched position. The fact that the boy was trying to avoid detection meant he had evil intentions and needed to be exorcised of this evil. From his crouched position, Kojo looked up to see the most evil-looking pair of eyes bearing down on him and wished he could disappear like a leprechaun. Teacher Kunta did not ask any questions like "Why do you look so scared?" "Why are you trying to avoid me?" or "Do you normally walk with a stoop?" Bullies always preyed on the scared and the boy looked scared. Kunta reached down, lifted the boy up by the collar like a paper toy, took him to the classroom, called for the biggest little boys of the class to hold his extremities, laid him over a table, and commenced flogging him. Kojo did not utter a sound. He had endured the baranzu, and this cane was a poor imitation. This was class 1, the noisiest class of the school, but the room was deathly quiet. After the whipping, Kojo walked away nonchalantly to the surprise of the audience of little people. He noiselessly cursed

the teacher and vowed to exact vengeance someday.

Mrs. Kunta was a calm, cultured and wonderful mother of two. Her disposition and demeanor was the exact opposite of the husband, and it was hard to imagine that people of such opposite polarity would be involved in a marital union. The strange alliance was due to the time-honored promoter of unions, which sometimes turned ugly; arranged marriage. The woman had been betrothed to Kunta through the involvement of family, and she might have regretted every minute of it, for Kunta commenced bullying the wife from day one. It was not uncommon to hear him screaming and yelling at this woman and treating her as if she were one of his class one charges:

*"Lazy woman where is my food"*

*"You lay about in the house doing nothing whilst I work my butt off"*

*"Hey, why are my kids so filthy? "*

*"Village woman, when are you going to stop gossiping?"*

Co-tenants in their house claimed that they had had to intervene many times to prevent him from physically assaulting her. Then suddenly the behavior towards her changed. It was as if Kunta had had a spiritual epiphany, except that he was his same obnoxious self when it came to his relationship with other people. Then the truth filtered out. According to sources, Kunta had one day, come home from school during school hours. There he chanced upon the wife taking a nap in a sitting posture and commenced insulting the wife even after she complained of headache and dizziness. When his nagging would not stop, the wife yelled back. Sacrilege. No one talks back at Kunta, especially a woman. He started to physically assault the little woman. With no one around except Eno, the octogenarian who skipped the farm because of sickness. Kunta was going to finally teach the impertinent wife a lesson. He missed with a punch, tripped, and was planted on his behind. Noticeably angry, he rushed the wife, who had the easy task of sidestepping the lumbering giant. Again, he fell flat on his face, and again got up and rushed the cowering woman. Unbeknown to anybody in the house, Kojo was lurking behind some boxes in the house. He had heard the shouting match and had tiptoed into the house to inquire. He had since been quietly watching the unfair fight without being seen by either party. Kunta was now going bonkers; it appeared that he would strangle the woman if

only he could get his hands on her. Kojo sensing danger rolled a pestle behind the big man. Kunta stepped on it, toppled over, and smashed his right leg against the mortar. When he got back up, he could not stand on the leg. The man attacked and went down again. As he kept falling, he got progressively weaker. Like a prize-fighter, Kunta changed styles; from a boxer to a karate expert to a wrestler but with the same result; he kept visiting the canvas because he could not plant the injured leg. Eno, watching from the safety of her room rubbed her eyes to make sure she was not in a trance. A true apostolic church believer, she was convinced God had something to do with that. The Holy Spirit was the one that had rolled the pestle that changed the tide of the fight; because except for the intervention of God, there was no way that big, bully could be lifted up and repeatedly thrown down by the frail woman. Finally, his kneecaps raw from having visited the ground so often, Kunta threw in the towel, claiming he had some important business back in school and warning the wife to be ready for the next round. After that incident, Mrs. Kunta lost her fear of the husband. She in turn, was often at the throat of the husband with Kunta playing the role of peacemaker. Odd statements like the ones below began to emanate from Kunta's mouth:

"Dear, can't we discuss matters without your always flaring up"?

"Be patient sweetheart".

"Honey let us compromise more as a loving couple are supposed to do".

"Darling, the Bible says wives should submit to their husbands you know".

Hitherto the words 'dear, darling, sweet, be patient' were never in the lexicon of Teacher Kunta.

The humiliation by the wife was not the end of the troubles of Teacher Kunta. Unknown to him, his most formidable adversary was the little bag-of-bones he thrashed that sunny afternoon in class 1. The Tamale transplant never forgave him for the ferocious whipping he gave him, for Kojo began to plan to exact vengeance as soon as he was let go. The teachers of Tamale never beat anyone without a reason. Kunta had beaten him without telling him his crime. He knew that "Vengeance is the Lord's", but the Lord was too slow for him.

Mrs. Kunta usually dried the family's clothes on a clothesline outside the house, and she got them back inside the house before nightfall. This observation was not lost on Kojo. On the clothesline, dried and ready to be folded and ironed were Mr. Kunta's school accoutrements, black shorts, white shirt, white singlet, and brown underwear. Kojo gathered the driest and most potent 'Poison Ivy' aka appéa. He then added a little bit of mesewa, the tropical strain of the notorious Jalapeno pepper. He kept the mixture of the two drugs for a week to ensure that the potency was at its zenith. Stealthily, he sprinkled just a little bit of the stuff onto the shorts, and the underwear; too much and the one folding or ironing the clothes would be the one affected. Soon enough a figure showed up and began gathering the dried clothes. The concoction of appéa and mesewa worked with a delayed release principle. With the proper measured dose, it took a while before it started working. The next day, Mr. Kunta swaggered to school assembly in his usual mean disposition. As he bellowed in his scary voice, he also occasionally dabbed at his bottom. Towards the end of the assembly, he was beginning to scratch his buttocks area with more frequency. To scratch is to spread, and soon enough the bully was tearing at his buttocks, and even private part in an obscene manner. Then the realization hit him that he was dealing with appéa. He roared to the audi-

ence asking for information about this treasonous crime, whilst promising to soon find out the perpetrators and flog them until kingdom come. Finally, he did what he should have done five minutes earlier; sprint towards home. The children and even the colleague teachers could not restrain themselves and burst out laughing. Kunta was a monster. Wild stories and rumors, many of them fabricated began to swirl around him. One story was that, on the way from farm, he had met a boy who failed to relieve him of the heavy load he was struggling with. The next day during class, he had a dialogue with that kid as follows:

Teacher Kunta: How many people did Jesus feed on the Sermon on the Mount?

Kid: 5000

Kunta: Name them.

Perhaps, sensing the animus of the people, Teacher Kunta eventually left town. Rumors had it that he was fired, but it was later found that he had been transferred to a much bigger town called Atebubu.

# The Fear of the Cross

O funu was Kojo's distant cousin. Ofunu who lived in Atebubu was a certified dunce. Kojo was appreciative of the fact that Ofunu was such a dimwit because he could always point to him as someone worse off academically in the family. Ofunu's father was a Muslim so he enrolled his son in a Makaranta, the Islamic equivalent of primary school. When he was in the Makaranta, Ofunu got the following results:

*Maths = 3%*

*English = 5%*

*Science = 2%*

*Social sciences = 1%*

*Koranic studies = 12%*

Apparently, the Biblical edict "Save the rod and spoil the child" was adhered to by Muslims, and Ofunu was frequently whipped very well. The father upon advice took him to a government

school where he managed to increase his scores by one full percentage point across board as seen in the following results:

*Maths = 4%*

*English = 6%*

*Science = 3%*

*Social sciences = 2%*

No amount of beatings could cure this boy of his bone headedness. The father was extremely disappointed. He decided to try him in a Catholic school. The first term, Ofunu received the following scores.

*Maths = 90%*

*English = 93%*

*Science = 95%*

*Social sciences = 89%*

*Bible Knowledge = 99%*

His parents could not believe it. His friends could not believe it. In fact, no one could believe it. The biggest surprise was his score

in Bible Knowledge because he did not own a Bible. They asked him how he managed to excel as he did, and he said:

"When I saw the picture in the classroom of a man nailed on the cross, I knew that the teachers in this school do not play". The fear of the cross is truly the beginning of wisdom.

# Examination Preparation

P reparation was the key word when it came to Examinations, and the the Common Entrance Examination was no different. Finally, Kojo was about to go to secondary school, but he had to take the dreaded Common Entrance Examination. The word 'Examination' has always been unpleasant at any level of school life. However, it is down¬right frightening during the earlier years in elementary school and Secondary school. This is especially true for external examinations in Ghana, Nigeria and across the whole of Africa. The word 'common' is a misnomer because there was nothing common about the examination. In fact, the uncommon Common Entrance examination had the right to proclaim itself as the most significant event in the life of a person, be it child or adult because this examination mostly determined a person's life trajectory. External examinations were accorded due respect and merited good preparation. As a result, most elementary schools organized special classes to teach candidates how to study for this life-changing event. The candidates were taught the rudiments of Arithmetic and English

sentence construction.  In the Saito schools aka 'schools in villages and the deprived areas of the cities and towns', the exchanges during this special preparatory classes could be interesting, other times banal and on a few occasions hysterically hilarious as captured below:

Teacher: How old is your father?

Kwame: He is 6 years.

Teacher: What? How is this possible?

Kwame: He became father only when I was born.


Teacher: Ama, go to the map and find North America

Ama: Here it is

Teacher: Correct. Now who discovered America?

Class: Ama


Teacher: Kofi, how do you spell 'crocodile'?

Kofi: K-R-O-KO-D-I-A-L

Teacher: No, that is wrong

Kofi: Maybe that is wrong, but you asked me how I spell it.


Teacher: Kojo, what do you call a person who keeps talking when

no one is interested?

**Kojo:** A teacher

**Teacher:** Construct a sentence using the word sugar

**Adwoa:** I drank tea this morning.

**Teacher:** Where is the word sugar?

**Adwoa:** My mom buys the tea with sugar already in it.

**Teacher:** What do you call mosquitoes in your language?

**Abu:** We do not call them. They come on their own.

**Teacher:** Name the nation people hate most

**Kojo:** Exami-nation...

**Teacher:** One day our country will be corruption free. What tense is that?

**Ray:** Future impossible tense

**Teacher:** Our topic for today is Photosynthesis. What is photo-synthesis class?

**Fiifi:** Photosynthesis is our topic today.

**Teacher:** Kobby is climbing a tree to pick some mangoes. Can

anyone begin the sentence with Mangoes?

**Ashkar:** Mangoes, Kobby is coming to pick you...

**Teacher:** How can we keep our school clean all the time?

**Okai:** By staying at home all the time.

**Teacher:** Ama has 30 cubes of sugar. She eats 20. What does she have?

**Adjo:** Diabetes.

**Teacher:** To change centimeters to meters you?

**Lasisi:** Take out the 'centi'.

**Teacher:** Kofi's father has five beer bottles in his right hand and four in the left hand. What does he have?

**Komla:** A drinking problem.

**Teacher:** Who is a meteorologist?

**Santo:** The driver of a metro bus

**Teacher:** Mr. Allotey plays the Piano. Who is he?

**Jaga:** He is a Pianist.

**Teacher:** Manangagwa lives in the capital. Who is he?

**Dudu:** He is a capitalist.


**Teacher:** Each one in the class shall mention one difference between a goat and a sheep.

**Lasisi:** The goat when you use it for soup it tastes waaaaow but the sheep when u use it for soup it does not taste waaaaow!

**Aidoo:** Goats give soup perfume especially the boy goat, but sheep do not give soup perfume.

**Kotey:** A goat can cross a road wisely, but the sheep is very foolish and walk slow on the road.

**Adzimahe:** A goat has a sharp brake, but a sheep does not have sharp brake.

**Oppong:** Goat head smells good, but sheep head does not smell at all.

**Frimpong:** Goat is stubborn, but sheep is humble.

**Roberto:** Goat can jump and turn 360° but sheep cannot jump and turn 360°.

**King:** The goat cry pobebe pobeee but sheep cries berh berh.

**Teacher:** We are going to do similes. We went over these exercis-

es last week. Therefore, each one should remember and answer one question only.

**Teacher:** A journey of a thousand miles.........

**Yaw:** begins with a bus fare.

**Teacher:** A bird in the hand.......

**Sarpong:** can be used for soup much more quickly than the one in the bush.

**Teacher:** Birds of the same feathers.......

**Bonu:** confuse the owner

**Teacher:** A friend in need......

**Boat:** cries for help

**Teacher:** Half a loaf......

**Kingsley:** does not satisfy hunger

**Teacher:** Those who live in glass houses.......

**Castro:** do not need mirrors

**Teacher:** A hungry man.......

**Torwudzo:** eats fast.

**Teacher:** Charity begins at.........

**Oti:** Seko?

**Teacher:** No, it is 'home'. Charity begins at home

**Oti:** Sir, my home is in Seko.

The exchanges were hilarious, but the preparations were serious. Past questions, aka paskos were the fulcrum of the preparations because they served as the truest measures of their readiness to the examination. When the children's knowledge markedly improved, they were given the past questions as a means of showing them the nuances and style of the examination. After that, they were shown how to write their names, shade their names, and shade their answers in the multiple-choice sections. The young boys and girls would be taking their first external exam; thus, jitters were a real problem. On 'D' day, those in the villages traveled to bigger venues in the towns and cities, and some in the cities moved to different and bigger venues. There was a real concern for jitters, for such changes in environment caused even more frayed nerves. Thus, smart kids with less resistance to nerves failed whilst relaxed dumbos that did not care a hoot about going to secondary school sometimes scraped through.

# The Serengeti March

Question. How many wildebeests take part in the annual cyclical journey in the Serengeti park for food and water? Answer. One and a half million. Every year wildebeests take part in a journey of 1,800 miles spanning multiple countries in a frantic search for food and water. The clockwise procession takes the clumsy but gentle beasts from the Serengeti through Ngorongoro to the Masai Mara back to the Serengeti. Thirst, exhaustion, hunger, and crocodiles take a frightful toll. It is said that 250,000 of these placid beasts perish on the journey. Thus, the migration can be likened to a death march. The alternative for the wildebeest is to not migrate. If there is no migration, about 50% of the beasts will perish, for the animals cannot survive for a year without nourishment. Ironically on this annual march, 600,000 new calves are born! Therefore, the journey is really a life march; for why many individuals are lost, the community of wildebeests survives and thrives. Thus, the credo

for these wild beasts is move or die. In Ghana, the journey of the children through the school system is not fraught with the same dangers as the wildebeests, but the result is the same. For why in the school world thousands graduate and leave the system, tens of thousands of adolescents join the system to replenish and add to what was lost. These younger adults seek knowledge the same way the wildebeests seek nourishment. For both wildebeest and child, the alternative of not marching is the same, death because lack of knowledge for a society is tantamount to death.

So, after so much struggle, so much angst, so much work and some luck, an army of children, tens of thousands strong, marched in unison to rejuvenate, replenish, and populate school campuses across the length and breadth of the nation.

*Onward Children soldiers!*

*Marching as to war,*

*With the flag of Ghana.*

*Going on before.*

*God the mighty master,*

*Leads against the foe,*

*Forward into battle,*

*See, His banners go!*

*Onward Children soldiers!*

*Marching as to war,*

*With the flag of Ghana.*

*Going on before.*

That was the song in their hearts and lips as children from the nooks and crannies of the country joined the march to their new campuses. In this procession were the accountants, architects, bankers, businessmen, civil servants, clergymen, diplomats, doctors, engineers, entrepreneurs, immigration officers, judges, lawyers, lecturers, military officers, nurses, pilots, police officers, politicians, scientists, teachers, town planners, and a 'who is who' of the future leadership of the country. Every region was represented, every city was included, every town was part of it, every village celebrated it, and every cottage watched it. Ethnicities and creeds were not left out. Every Kofi was there, every Musah was there, every Nii was there, every Adjo was there, and Kojo was there.

# THE

# HIGH SCHOOL

# YEARS

# Gari

R eady-to-eat-meal anytime, anywhere, anyhow is a perfect description of Gari. Kojo was well prepared to survive in boarding school because he had in his chop box, the most im¬portant food to supplement the notoriously inadequate dining hall meals, Gari. This cereal is unquestionably the best 'Student Companion' when it comes to food in boarding schools in Ghana, Nigeria and beyond. The cassava derivative is indeed a faithful friend indeed, for it answers the call to duty when hunger comes knocking at twelve midnight. Gari is found practically everywhere in the environment of a boarding school. It is found in pockets, bags, pans, jars, tins, cans, olonkas, konkos, boxes and chop boxes; and it thrives under conditions that can cause the best-preserved foods to go bad. In the dormitory, no one has witnessed this food being thrown out on account of it going putrid, rotten, or contaminated. This food could be a close second to honey in terms of longevity.

However, gari's popularity is not merely because it has staying power. As Mr. Ayoade, the loquacious Nigerian tutor, a serious

partaker of this 'mother of all cereals' put it with such poetic elegance,

'Gari's utility is the reason for its ubiquity'.

It can be eaten in more forms than can be enumerated. It can be eaten with or without sugar, with or without salt, with or without soup, with or without milk, with or without water, cooked or uncooked and it can be eaten with nothing. Its yeast-like ability to bloat the stomach makes it a favorite of cash-challenged individuals because a spoonful of the stuff with a glass of water can quickly fill one up for hours. And of course, gari assuages hunger when one is mining; that is, studying at late night especially during exam periods.

Gari transcends ethnic and national boundaries too. Gari kneaded into soft and succulent eba with the accompaniment of okra stew, by a Yoruba woman, serves the purpose of the sumptuous evening supper. The Avetime mother of three turns the same "hot water and gari" combo into mouth-watering 'gari foto' with an aroma that can persuade the hungry and angry husband hanging out at the palm wine parlor to come home. The Ashanti spinster with a limited budget just adds a small quantity of hot water, kneads the stuff into a dough, grinds pepper, onion, tomatoes

into a paste, adds koobi and calls it gari fufu; the hard pressed city man adds room temperature water to the stuff, warms any available stew or soup and his gari is ready to go. The preparation of this food does not always require cooking else, how is a student going to take the stuff in a dorm? With water it turns into a mushy mass to be eaten with shitto and sardines; double the water, add milk and sugar and the same quantity of gari turns into 'soakings', the number one student favorite. Then is another delicious gari-derived food, yoké gari. This preparation requires beans as the partner, a resource that is not readily available in school dorms else, it could have been a major contender for the best dorm food. But yoké gari is usually sold close enough to boarding houses and other student hangouts to merit mention.

With such versatility, gari is not merely a food; it is a food support group. Only a crazy form one student would report at the boarding house without gari, for it is the major currency that is used to bribe seniors from inflicting harassment. As the popular saying goes: 'a form one student without gari is like Africa without Madagascar'.

# DASS Characters

Secondary Schools in Ghana come in various shapes, sizes, and backgrounds. But they all had the same structure of five years for the Ordinary level, and 2 additional years for the A-Level. The train that was Dwamena Akenten Second¬ary School aka DASS chugged along as Form 2 blurred into Form 3. Like any passenger train, some dropped off and others jumped on. New faculty came to DASS, among whom was the eccentric Mathematics teacher, who used the word 'actual' so often it replaced his preferred monikers of 'Bolaman, and Alonzo Thiefman'. Actual was an excellent mathematics teacher who replaced another excellent and immensely popular figure Kenneth Yeboah aka Masken.

Masken walked with a perceptible limp. One Saturday during entertainment hour, Masken watched transfixed with horror as a competition to produce the student that could best mimic his walking style unfolded before his eyes. Student after student paraded doing their best paraplegic imitation, some dragging the

feet as if Masken was a cripple.

The hilarious handling of the 'Physics topic Diffusion' using the analogy of flatulence by the Physics mas¬ter Mr. Amoah aka Ida aka Either, was the stuff of which legends are made. He began thus: "Suppose someone gives bad air at the corner there"— Either paused to make sure the statement had maximum effect and then continued, "even though there is no air blowing there, I can still smell it here. This is diffusion." Kojo, who usually polluted that corner, grimaced as Either gazed in his direction.

Sundiata the history teacher suffered in the hands of his students. A stammerer who had overcome his challenge by vocalizing words slowly, he used to pose the question for which he was most famous.

"What ...led ...to ...the rise ...of ...Ghana?" There was a long pause after each word; thus, it took about twice as long as the average reader would take.

Mr. La the geography master was notorious for dictating voluminous amounts of notes. Stu¬dents did not look forward to geography exams because they involved a lot of reading. Adom, unable to study all the material at one of his exams, decided to tip, that is, memorize a few carefully selected topics to the exclusion

of others. Unfortunately, none of his tips showed up. Therefore, he wrote a note at the top of the exam sheet: "I am very sorry, but I did not study the topics here, below are the topics I studied." Adom then regurgitated the topic he had "chewed." Mr. La had a sense of humor. He graded Adom's essay and gave maximum grade to it but gave a zero to each topic he skipped.

Mandibles came on board as the biology teacher in Form 3. In his white shirt, black pants, red tire, white belt, protruding belly, and unmistakably prominent square jaws, Mandibles cut a comedic figure. The first topic he treated, the anatomy of insects, which of course included the mandible or jaw, became the source of his nickname.

Ayoade, a verbose Nigerian was the most charismatic of the bunch. It was a big surprise that Ayoade was made to teach French instead of English literature. His favorite phrase was "Why are you are looking so morose and melancholic". He spoke French with a funny accent, but he could rival Shakespeare when it came to romancing the English language. Ayoade did not have a nickname, maybe because his Nigerian name was a nickname.

O'Bad was the shorthand as well as moniker of the assistant headmaster. A generation older than the other tutors, it was dif-

ficult to associate a nickname to the old-fashioned O'Bad. O'Bad spoke English with an accent and diction that would have made the English royal family proud, and he insisted that his students do likewise—a tall order because many of his charges were seriously English-challenged.

On top of the food chain was the headmaster Mr. Ababio. Mr. Ababio was a disciplinarian but a benevolent dictator who tempered justice with mercy, so to speak. The great man was given the moniker Sofo because he schooled in Prempeh College aka Sofoline University. Mr. Ababio had an interesting behavior worthy of mention. Standing at obscure corners and walking furtively behind or alongside students on pitch-dark nights, this modern-day Sir Arthur Conan Doyle was able to eavesdrop on mostly idle boy-girl chatter from which he sometimes got wind of potentially subversive stuff. During Sunday church sermons, the am¬ateur intelligence obtained on such reconnaissance missions was made to appear as if it was divinely acquired. Soon enough his modus operandi was found out, and an alert system was devised to warn students of his presence. A shout of 'Sofo' sent students scurrying into the nearest hole, so to speak.

Latin was not the most popular subject, and Laudamus the Lat-

in master Mr. Kankam, was not a jolly popular fellow. Laudamus got his moniker the day he introduced the Latin prayer 'Te Deum Laudamus'. Latin was not necessarily a tough one, but the idea that it was not spoken anywhere save perhaps the Vatican made studying it with enthusiasm diffi¬cult. Latin was a language with an attitude. Like French, its verbs had to be conjugated, but its nouns also had to undergo a metamorphosis of some sorts called declension. The double whammy of conjugation and declension gave Latin a notoriety all its own. The Romans of yore were well-cultured people. They addressed each other with respect and decorum, and they expected even their inanimate possessions, such as tables, to be addressed appropri¬ately. It was a hard sell for Mr. Kankam to tell students that they had to be mindful of their language when addressing inanimate objects.

A 'table' is conjugated as follows:

Mensa, Mensa, Mensam, Mensarum, Mensis, Mensis.

Laudamus: 'Mensa is when I, as a first person, am talking to a table; again, Mensa is when you, as a second person, are talking to a table; and Mensam is when he or she, in the third person, is talking to a table.

In the novel My Early Life, the autobiography of Winston Chur-

chill, the Englishman ex¬pressed similar misgivings about learning a dead language like Latin. Until he started doing Latin, Kojo had no idea what Mr. Churchill's problem was about. Now he understood the Englishman's reluctance to address tables albeit appropriately.

Kojo: Sir, but I never talk to a table, I do not want to talk to a table, and I do not intend to ever talk to a table. At this stage, Laudamus could do little but join in the fun of a befuddled Form 1 class. Teach¬ing Latin was a dirty job, too bad somebody had to do it. Nevertheless, he decided to use humor to wriggle out of the situation.

Laudamus: Why don't you appropriately address the dining hall table then? It might turn your 'green-green' to 'red-red'.

Kojo was convinced that the Romans ruled the world more by brain than brawn; for if Roman kids grew up into this conjugation and declension world without complaint, then they really deserved to rule the universe.

As expected, students had their share of monikers. Form 1 was the most likely class for one to get a nickname if one ever got one. Senior students were always dreaming up ways to embarrass Form 1 students.

Saturday night is the most fun night in boarding school because Saturday night is entertainment night. There is usually a plethora of programs to enliven the evening such as dancing, music, movies, spelling bee, poetry, and comedy. One inauspicious Saturday night, Kojo was randomly summoned to the stage to conjugate the French word etre. Etre, which translates as 'to be,' is probably the first French verb a student learns about in secondary school. Kojo was always doing his best Monsieur Mwanga, the Form 1 French master impersonation, so this task was going to be easy. Everyone yawned when Kojo mounted the podium thinking how lucky he was to have gotten a task so easy. Quickly and with a swagger he went to the front. Up there on the podium, Kojo realized there were more people than he thought. With so many eyes fixated on him he froze, and began dishing out good entertainment the like of which had never been given before:

*"Je suis,*

*tu suis,*

*il suis ..."*

Pandemonium broke out! The Form 5 students giggled, Form 4 students hooted with joy, and Form 3 students cackled with laughter; but Form 2 students did not hold back. They screamed

with delight and high-fived each other. Kojo, drenched in sweat even in that cold November night, underwent this baptism of humiliation. Fellow form one students, aka homos could not help but join this carnival of laughter as their classmate was made to conjugate etre repeatedly. For a few weeks after this day, Kojo was called 'Je suis'. When people started calling him Jesus, the Christian Fellowship protested the blasphemy, and the nickname died.

# Favorite School Meal

Thursday is a very ordinary day indeed. For unlike Monday, it is not wished against; and unlike Friday, it is not wished for. Thus, it is neither unloathed nor unloved. But Thursday was a notable day in DASS because it was 'Ato Day', and Ato was the caviar of boarding school food. On this day at lunch, the dining hall did not buzz with its usual frenetic activ¬ity. Rather, students sat stolidly like pilgrims before the appearance of a prophesied spiritual specter. Attendance registered 100 percent come rain or shine and checking for late comers was an exercise in futility. Usually, some seniors stayed out of the hall and instructed their batmen to send their meals to their dorm rooms because of schoolwork and other chores; some juniors also skipped lunch for reasons of ill health or disdain for the item on the menu. Not on Thursday, for Thursday was ato day.

Ato, over which best friends parted on disagreement as to who got the bigger pieces.

Spectator, the only event to rival and even beat INTAKO in terms

of spectators.

Kokoo ne adua, the uncrowned heavyweight champion of the gastronomic kingdom in boarding schools in Ghana.

Kekee, over which boy-girl dates were not honored because of scheduling snafus.

'Red-red', the only food with a color code.

Pekyee, the food with more nicknames than the tutor with the most nicknames in any school.

These were all one and the same food, 'ripe plantain and beans.'

Ato, the caviar of boarding schools, was more than a food; it was a belief with a following. It was a belief that food could bring unity and joy to people; the happy faces of students as they munched on those succulent and juicy pieces were the clearest testament to that.

Juniors and seniors united in worshipping this food of the gods. Bad deeds such as rebelling against authority, strife between sporting teams, and juniors defying seniors were guaranteed not to take place on Thursday days. Simply put, no one wanted to miss their plateful of ripe plantain and beans or to detract from the joy of taking it. On good ato days, the pieces were bigger and softer, and the beans dripped with red oil, and the partakers of

the meal had lips that glistened like women straight out of the boudoir.

Those were the pre-cholesterol days when good food could be enjoyed without the constant homily of blocked arteries and hypertension. The most powerful persons in the dining room, bar none, were the servers. Servers were the juniors that dispensed the food, making sure to give equal pieces to each student. The pieces were assumed to be approximately equal for the slices of plantain were supposed to have been equally subdivided by the kitchen staff. However, a big plantain was sliced in two equal parts, and so was a small one. Therefore, some of the pieces were more equal than others were, and therein lay the power of the servers. A server could heap the plates of his favorites with the biggest and juiciest portions; conversely, he could serve the scrawniest pieces to people he was not fond of. Most stiffed students would nurse their anger and suffer in silence, but not Kojo. Kojo would protest and threaten the server if he felt the pieces he was served were not to his liking. After receiving the pieces that merited his approval, he would commence eating, sans spoon, sans fork, and sans the mandatory prayers. Kojo had an

irritating habit. He would sometimes dip his hand into the main bowl for the table, pull out a piece, start eating from the bowl and invite the server to follow suit. The server knew better than to do that, for he would have been skinned alive after Kojo left. Even bad ato was better than other non-ato meals. Bad ato could mean a variety of things; it meant the pieces were not well ripened, were skinny and less tender, and/or the beans stew did not drip with enough palm oil.

Yam-and-nkontomire stew was popular, and so was yam-and-palm-nut soup, but none of them portrayed the pure joy captured on faces of students on Thursday afternoons. Ato enjoyed gastronomic folk-hero status. In many boarding schools in the country, Ato was to students what fufu was to the village folk. A disadvantage of fufu in this popularity contest was that fufu had variety and therefore lacked a distinct personality; there was fufu and abenkwan, fufu and nkatenkwan, fufu and abunabunu—a.k.a. green-green—fufu and aponkye nkra-kra, etc.; so when one is invited to a fufu meal, one did not quite know what to expect. Ato did not have this disadvantage of being paired with so many suitors, for ato always meant "ripe plantain and beans." In other words, ato was a completed statement while fufu was not.

Among those that came to worship at the altar of Ato the food god, was the conspicuous white face of Robert Oprandy. The ubiquitous American Peace Corps volunteer had discovered this delectable delight and made sure to return from his trips to Kumasi and other environs before noon on Thursdays. Oprandy ensconced himself in a corner where he meted out justice to a plateful of Ato while trying desperately to appear invisible. Nevertheless, even a white man licking his bare fingers while students from villagers were delicately balancing cutlery did not elicit enough curiosity to distract from the enjoyment of Ato.

# Robin Hood of Prempeh

Unapologetically, Prempeh College is a great school. And it is a gated community. Securi¬ty personnel operated the gates to prevent unde-sirables from entering and causing mischief, but an equally important function of the walls was to pre¬vent students from sneaking out. It was a tough assignment preventing young men of good athletic ability from scaling the walls. The school imposed severe sanctions to deter the students from venturing outside the confines, but these were not enough to stop Boro.Peterborough aka Boro was an unassuming Form 3 student with the looks and demeanor of a choirboy. Either for reasons of claustrophobia or for a sense of adventure, Boro sought ways to sneak out of campus at his choosing. This school Robin Hood was not the wall-scaling type; rather he was a genius at creating false passages that could elude detection by a king scout. When it came time for Boro to go out, he removed the false hedge or wall, and hey, presto, he was out. Kojo came

from a school with infinite reach, in other words, without walls. Not used to physical walls, he felt confined and hemmed in. It was a mental struggle for him to accept the fact that he was not in prison. Not long after he arrived at this glorified prison, he heard of the exploits of Boro and sought him out. After a couple of escapades to watch movies in Rivoli, the feeling of claustrophobia vanished. Kojo became good friends with Boro and helped him open more passageways. Boro's fame was at its apogee. Other boys that really needed to go out to see a girl or go to a hot new movie contacted Boro, who gladly led them out through a Boro highway, the name given to these passages. The school authorities heard of this labyrinth of highways that seemed to violate the sanctity of the hallowed grounds of Prempeh and vowed to close them down. Security guards and other security staff examined the wall to seal any illegal entrances. The authorities mounted sting operations that caught many students, but never came close to apprehending the architect. The legend of Boro received a boost when Mr. Kyere, a mathematics tutor and patron of the Christian fellowship, preached a sermon in which he entreated students to stop evil practices such as using Boro highways to abscond from campus. Hitherto the name Peterbor-

ough was underground lingo. It was merely whispered among the student body. Now through Koo Kyere, it had entered the lexicon of Prempeh College as a word of guile, rebelliousness, and freedom. Grudgingly, even six formers approached Boro for help when they wanted to sneak out. Finally, Rivoli, the nearest movie house, was only a false passageway away. If word got around that a good movie was showing, not even a Berlin Wall could stop Kojo and movie buffs like Borlai and Asaf from sneaking out. Boro never charged a dime for his services; the thrill of outwitting the school authorities was enough reward for this benign rebel. Boro highways were not the only way of escaping from campus. There was another even more nerve-tingling way of absconding from campus. This one indirectly involved religion. As is customary, devout Muslims dutifully offer their prayers without fail at sundown every day. The prayer sessions usually took about ten minutes, and this time interval provided an opportunity for students to walk through the gates in full glare of the guards. Fortunately, or unfortunately, the security guards that manned the points of entry to the campus were devout Muslims. Students take religion less seriously and are more apt to make a mockery of serious activities such as rituals and ablutions. For reasons unknown

to non-practitioners of the faith, a Muslim practitioner bobs the head up and down during prayers, not unlike the adult male lizard. This ritual always signaled that the security guards were in deep prayer and was thus the best time to walk out of the gate. It was a comedic spectacle to observe the guards doing this up and down bobbing prayer ritual even as students strolled through the hitherto Fort Knox-like manned gates. From the corner of his eye, Mallam Seidu could see the miscreants brazenly sauntering away. He would speed up the bobbing motion to finish praying quickly. Mallam was both a respected and feared figure. But that did not stop students from derisively waving at him as they made their exits. Mallam would sprint after the group as soon as he was done, but it was really a lost cause; he was too old to engage in a sprint with kids some young enough to be his grandsons. He did get lucky on occasion. The unfortunate chap would be smacked and then released; Mallam could not leave the gate unmanned and send the offender to the authorities. The culprit was more grateful for the smacks for it was a better alternative to being sent to Gyimah or Oso, who could go by the book and invoke a suspension for first offenders and a dismissal for repeat ones.

# Amazing Race

Very fast is an apt description of sprinters, after all sprinting means running very fast like a Sprinter bus. Of all the sports and events at a track meet, the apprehension, excitement, and anxiety of the 100 x 4 relay is second to none. Aficionados of track will tell you that relay races are notorious for one thing, the baton exchange. An average team that seamlessly synchronizes the exchanges may triumph over a team of individual Olympians. The death sentence of a relay race is the dropping of the baton. In a sport in which winning and losing is calculated in the milliseconds, no team that drops the baton will ever be able to pick it up and come back to win a competitive relay race.

To secondary schools in Ghana, Inter Collegiate Athletic Competition aka INTERCO was more important than the World Cup and the Olympics games combined. INTERCO is the ultimate games of Secondary school sports, and the anticipation for the day is beyond comprehension! That year's one was even better because

never in living memory had so many quality athletes competed against each other on one tartan track! That day, Kumasi sports stadium was stacked with the best sprinters 'money cannot buy'. Like the previous years and many other years before, Prempeh College and Opoku Oware, the two goliaths of Ashanti sports were in contention. The competition at this stage was a virtual dead heat between the two adversaries. Therefore, the anticipation for the final race, which is the 4 × 100 meters relay was out worldly. A couple of false starts combined to make the tension so thick it could be cut with a knife.

The baton demands to be respected, because to disrespect it increases the odds of dropping it and dropping it signifies doom.

The unbelievable Prempeh line up was as follows:

1.    Ntiforo aka Santo

2.    Stan Allotey aka Speedometer.

3.    Ohene Frimpong aka King.

4.    Kwadwo Frimpong Ansah aka KAFA.

The OWASS quartet looked even more potent with more high-profile stars.

1.    Sandy Osei Agyemang aka Sandy.

2.    Fokuo aka FOKs

3.     Rex Brobbey aka Abigi

4.     Ohene Karikari aka Sahara.

Each and every one of the eight athletes that lined up for both schools had represented the nation one time or another.

Sahara had recently won the 100-meter dash at the All-Africa Games. And the handsome speedster Sandy was the previous year's 100-meter dash winner. Go figure.

There was enough talent that auspicious Saturday afternoon at the Kumasi Sports stadium to threaten the African and common-wealth records. That was the INTERCO aka INTAKO, the Olym-pics of secondary school track and field in Ghana.


KPOM sounded the starter's gun. Sandy shot off in his typical long looping strides, but try as he did, he could not shake off Santo. The batons were seamlessly handed over. The race was now between Foks and Speedometer, and within a few strides Prempeh had inched ahead as Speedometer neatly handed over to King. Abigi made up the grounds lost, caught King, and now OWASS was ahead. When the penultimate runner Foks flawless-ly handed the baton to the current Africa's sprint king Sahara, everyone thought that this one was in the bag for OWASS, forgetting that there was one round more to go before any celebration could begin. A collective gasp of .... oooh.... reverberated even as the baton slipped from the grasp of Sahara and hit the tartan track. The unthinkable had happened. As if responding to the conductor of an orchestra, the screaming bedlam that was OWASS froze. A few blinked back momentary tears as they stared into space, not bearing to look at the unfolding disaster. Meanwhile the 'Against' crowd led by Prempeh students started doing cartwheels. With this kind of providential accident only divine intervention could stop them from winning the race and subsequently the championship. When a baton impacts the ground, it bounds up in a many random ways. It can bounce left, right, sideways, up or it may even refuse to bounce up. In its bouncing escapades, there is an exceedingly small but non-zero probability that it may come back to where it belonged; and the latter path was what this sacred piece of wood chose. However, the momentary lapse was enough to break his stride. By the time the baton got back in his grasp, Sahara was the tail of a contiguous speeding mass of humanity with the Prempeh's KAFA as the head. Sahara was running so fast. The chest was heaving, and perspiration was blinding him. In fact, he was going the fastest he had gone

in his sprinting life. The 100-metre world record would be his if only they could measure his speed for this part of the race. He had made up lost ground and beaten everybody except KAFA. With not much real estate left KAFA breasted the tape winning by an almost zero body length. Close but no cigar. Pandemonium is too weak a word to describe the scene that ensued. Spectators surged towards the field to catch a glimpse of the athlete that had beaten the celebrated African champion right before their very eyes. Others furiously rubbed their eyes to see if their retinae and pupils were in alignment. Alas, on the faces of OWASS students was abject unbelief. What ignominy! That with even an African champion, they would lose to their worst adversary. But finally, the memories of the previous year's heartbreak had been exorcised and OWASS was made to lick its wounds until the next year in the never-ending contest for regional athletics supremacy.

# Tech at Last, Tech at Last

Whispering the speech of the great man, Kojo beamed as he surveyed the great campus of Kwame Nkrumah University of Science and Technology aka KNUST aka Tech. He was not alone.

'Tech at Last, Tech at Last 'Thank God Almighty, I am in Tech at last.'

were the words on the lips of everyone that got accepted into KNUST, the citadel of the brainy of the quantitative variety. For most, the holy grail of scholastic achievement was on the verge of attainment.

The long-streamed official names were for the politicians to hyperventilate about. For regular folk, it was Tech. Even though he had been on this campus numerous times; from his elementary school days in Kotei to his current vacation job in BRRI he had always been overawed. Nevertheless, it looked more awesome today if that was possible. From the vantage point at Tech junction, the tall buildings in the distance, engulfed by the low billowing clouds seemed to want to scrape the heavens. Now he under-

stood why they got their name. They were so tall they scraped the skies. Slowly he made his way toward the campus, soaking in the scenery and wondering why it was taking him so long to get to one tall edifice that could be made out from afar. Boy was the campus massive! Prempeh was big, but it was a tiny speck when compared with the Tech campus. It would be two weeks before he would be an official resident in this great kingdom with the rights and privileges of a resident, but he walked the grounds with a certain pride and aloofness as if he owned a piece of this prime real estate. "Resident," he muttered softly; the thought was enough to flood his skin with goose pimples. It seemed like he was having a spiritual epiphany. Republic Hall was his allotted residence; an older hall with an annex that towered ten floors off the ground. It was where he would spend the blissful days ahead. How he longed to have gone to Unity Hall, aka Continental, aka Konti! Konti was the newest hall to be added to the university's infrastructure. It had two high-rises that stood adjacent to each other with an intervening courtyard and boasted the biggest pond on campus. Everything about Konti was modern and exquisite, making it the consensus first-choice residence of first year students. The process of assigning the halls was supposed

to be random, so some got in Konti and some did not; he did not. Seeing Konti again evoked memories of a field trip that he undertook years earlier when he was in Form 2 in DASS. The group of thirty students had been touring the campus. Konti was always on the itinerary of touring groups. The tourists mesmerized by the sheer size of this goliath of edifices, were also being observed from above. Lo and behold, one of the residents came down and expressed a wish in hosting a couple of students. The selection of these two chaps was the prerogative of the host, who promptly chose classmates Kojo and his friend, both snappy dressers. The man rolled the red carpet and gave the two lucky boys the treat of their lives. They were taken up the elevators to the top floor into his room where they were feted like royalty. The starry-eyed visitors could not stop gawking at the concrete jungle that was Konti, with its fast elevators, well-manicured lawns, gardens, sparkling pond, and five-star-quality dining service. From the apex of the skyscraper, they surveyed the expanse below and felt powerful because they towered over every living thing as far as the eye could see. For those fleeting moments, the tiny little juniors felt like monarchs of all they could survey. Later, they went down to have lunch in the company of other

doting university students. The beverage was like nothing he had tasted before. Cold, yummy and nectarous chocolate. After he finished his cup, he did an Oliver Twist impersonation and asked for more. The pantry staff obliged and brought another cup, then he asked for another, and then another. When the shy friend joined the fray, the pantry man went beyond the call of duty and brought down a whole jar. The dining hall dissolved into laughter at the sheer audacity of the two little boys that were behaving as if they belonged. When it was time for them to leave, Kojo vowed that he was coming back, if only for more cold choco- late. The recollection of that story brought a smile to his face. He made it. That was at least six years ago. He was proud of himself, his uncle was proud of him, his mother was proud of him, and his grandfather would have been proud of him. Even Reverend Martin Luther King would not have minded a plagiarized version of his great speech.

*Tech at Last,*

*Tech at Last,*

*Thank God Almighty,*

*I am in Tech at last.*

# Ananse's COVID Protocols

**X**ylophone, gong-gong and fontomfrom music was the preserve of the rich, and Kwaku Ananse was the richest person on the planet. He had all the goodies money could buy - mansions, fleet of cars, private jets, yachts, servants, maids to mention but a few. When the wife Aso tapped him on the shoulder to wake him up in the morning, he nearly slapped her for interrupting his dream. In fact, he did not believe it was not a reality. In rage, he appeared before God with a complaint. Why would God not make dreams real? Ananse would not accept any explanation from God. Therefore, God assured him that from that day forward his dreams would become real. He thanked God and disappeared in no time. At home, Ananse boasted to Aso his wife how he was able to convince God to make his dreams real. Not long after that, Ananse who did not believe in COVID-19 and taunted those who did, lost his sense of taste and smell. He was persuaded by his wife to see a doctor only to find that he was COVID-19 positive. In no time, his condition deteriorated. He he recovered, he would observe

the was in constant pain. On his hospital bed Ananse swore that, if ever he recovered, he would observe the COVID-19 protocols with a vengeance. He came up with ANANSE COVID PROTOCOLS:

•Social distance is 12 instead of the CDC- recommended 6 feet.

•Triple masks in his home

•Sanitizer to replace all creams and lotions in his house.

•Also, to fully comply with the quarantine rules, he was going to be a monk and live away from everyone.

Ananse had become a strong advocate in the war against COVID-19. He promoted vaccinations in the African American and Latino communities. He caused to be painted on his walls the paraphrase from the Bible 'The Fool Says in his Heart, there is no COVID'.

His condition got very bad. The screaming was so much that the doctors decided to put him off his misery. Just as the doctor was about to pull the plug, his wife tapped him to wake him up. Ananse heaved a sigh of relief when he opened his eyes and realized it was a dream. He ran to God and begged him not to make dreams a reality.

# APPRECIATION

I really appreciate your reading my book. And I am sure there was more than one smile on your face! Please, let me know in FACEBOOK which part of the little book brought the biggest smile.

Below are my social media coordinates:

Friend me on Facebook:     www.facebook.com/michaelfrimpon

Follow me on Twitter:     www.twitter.com/michaelfrimpon

Subscribe to my blog:     www.blog.frimpon.com

Connect on LinkedIn:     www.linkedin.com/in/michaelfrimpon

# BIO

Michael Forson Frimpon is a mathematician, but writing is his joy. His literary works include "The Boy in the Oversized Smock", "The Boy in the Oversized Coat", and "Early School Memories". His current work KOJO'S HEYDAY, is an effort to infuse a little cheerfulness into these current mirthless COVID-19 days.

www.ingramcontent.com/pod-product-compliance
Lightning Source LLC
Chambersburg PA
CBHW070340130626
46556CB00007B/2952